Low Worm Diet
A novel

by
Chuck Redman

Cover Art by Ricky Congello
Interior Design by Vinnie Corbo

Published by Volossal Publishing
www.volossal.com

To Jilla, Josh and Rebecca

ONE

John Roberts never said a word against people marrying whomever they want. He only said that courts should stay out of it. Courts aren't in the business of deciding fundamental values, people are. In their own states, he said. Like Ohio. He said it in writing. It was published. John Roberts works for the Supreme Court. Glenn thinks his dissent was the greatest thing ever written, at least since *The Da Vinci Code*.

And Glenn's read a lot of dissents. One of them made him cry. Actually, he even cried during the picture, the one that's got twelve nominations and is the story of two women who should be able to marry each other if they want. John Roberts would probably have cried during that picture too, if he saw it, and maybe he did. Hollywood makes some pretty good pictures and makes a huge number of people cry and feel good about themselves and get into other people's heads and understand a little bit about why people do the things they do to each other and people walk out of the theaters probably a little less inclined to hang on to their prejudices or start a war. Hollywood has also written most of the best symphony music composed in the past eighty years, which Glenn appreciates.

Hollywood's a grimy place, though. That's why the red carpet. Those celebrities need to get their tuxedos and shoes and dresses back to the rental agencies clean and in good shape. Not by midnight, but probably the next day. After The Oscars.

Glenn and John Roberts don't seem to care that much if the picture about the two women wins or not, but Vicky does. She's had the TV prattling since 3:15, while she knits through low-set reading glasses, and since the TV is thirty-two years old everything looks a little red but today especially. Glenn and Vicky's carpet is green but all afternoon it's had a reddish cast. Not so much during the commercials, though, unless it's a commercial for a red sporty sedan from Germany being driven all alone down a dark drippy avenue by that guy who talks to himself, but in metaphors. About how perfect his car is. When Glenn gets up from his lawn chair and squeezes himself, his sweater and his book through the streaky sliding glass door which needs oil and pulls off his sunglasses which don't, a commercial for that credit card, the new one that talks to you, is just finishing.

"Have I won anything?"

Vicky snorts. "You've won the privilege of sitting next to me," she says. "And keeping me company." Her needles have stalled and she's counting stitches with her finger. Through the drugstore lenses Vicky's eyes are enormous. Like King Kong's.

"Not best husband in a supporting role?"

"Mmmmh. Maybe next year, Hon. Get yourself a better publicist." Vicky can smile in the right direction without once taking her eyes off her yarn.

"Heh. Have they given out any of the big ones? Why do they—" Glenn stops and cocks his right ear toward the television. "That sounds like Tchaikovsky's—"

"Shhhh. They're doing Best Animated Short Film."

"Sweetheart, I don't think we even saw any of the Long—"

"Shhhh!"

"—Animated Whatever. Do you want anything from the kitchen?"

She shakes her head. "Okay, an apple. Sliced. With peanut butter." Glenn is awarded a single hazel glance, over dark plastic rims. He rolls off the couch, kitchenward. And by the time he gets back with their platter of snacks Vicky is looking at him with tragedy. But without blinks.

"What?"

She lets out a dying breath and deflates like a punctured tire on a lonely highway.

"What!"

"It would have been so nice," she says, "to have another couple over to watch the Oscars with. Get a pizza, make a salad. A bottle of wine."

Glenn suddenly looks like he's been aged many years by the makeup department in one of the big studios. "I know." That's his line. He plays a guy who just got diagnosed with something that the doctor had to look up on the internet. "Wull. We'll do it one of these weekends, maybe for the playoffs."

"Yeah. Sure. That's gonna happen."

"Wull—"

"So who's the couple that you like so much that you're just dying to have them over? And have a regular conversation like other human beings in this world? Hmmmh?"

"Wull, lots of couples. There's plenty."

"Who?"

"Do I have to say one now?"

Vicky blinks. The sour cream on Glenn's half-burrito melts. The TV extols, exults and exalts and the backyard shadows paw at the sliding glass door.

"Okay," says Glenn. For a long pause he's basically inert, but pairs of anatomical things stir. A set of wide lips bunch up, thin shoulders hunch and lungs expand. When a commercial for Buxom Burger comes on and the girl eating their new Spicy Pork Chow Mein Burger starts dripping juices all over herself and smiling, Glenn's eyes narrow. "What about the Weisslers? Keith and Kelly."

"That's who you want to invite?" Vicky is not unamused. "Hon, you almost had a nervous breakdown because she talked so much her filet got cold and she had to send it back. Twice, I think. And you thought he was a pantywaist."

"No, I thought he was a child molester. Okay, how about the Cletuses? Him and what's her name."

She shakes her head. "I don't think so. Clarice or something. It bothered you that they were too rich. And he was always bragging and saying how much things cost and you said we had nothing to one-up them with. I guess I wasn't too thrilled with them either."

Glenn bites his lower lip like James Cagney talking to coppers, and adds a sucking sound. "Yeah. Well look, there's always Harry and Diane."

"Divorced."

"The Fernandezes?"

"You mean the Hernandezes?"

"Nevermind. Tom and Peg?"

"No such couple."

"Somebody and Peg?"

She looks upward and after four seconds starts shaking her head as if cursing the day that popcorn ceilings were invented.

"Swell." He opens the book resting beside him on the couch and adjusts the bookmark in terms of the length by which it protrudes. It takes a bit of deliberation. "There was someone else I was gonna—"

"Meryl Streep and Morgan Freeman!"

"No, that wasn't it. I think they might be a little out of our league."

"No, smarty, they're presenting the Jean Hersholt Humanitarian Award. You."

Smirks must be good for the appetite. After eyeing his tortilla chips and guacamole for a couple seconds Glenn starts munching. "Are you gonna cook or we'll just pick up, or what?"

"It doesn't matter. We could go out. Depends on the couple."

"Hummel's?"

"Sure. Or Ponte Vecchio."

"Hummel's is quieter. Their prime rib wasn't so great last time, though."

"You were just getting over a sinus infection, you probably couldn't taste."

"I've gotta pick up some Bronchadine, I think I took the last, or maybe the next to the last—"

"I'm picking up my prescription tomorrow, I can get you some. Not 'til after lunch, though."

"While you're at it, can you get me a bottle of Hurry Up? I'm a little, you know."

"I bought prunes. And Bran Central cereal."

"I know but. I need something a little stronger."
When rewarmed beans and cheese sit for a while, they're pretty good at clinging to forks, and need very little direct supervision. Glenn's eyes are free to stare into space. "Whatever happened to that gal you liked even though she had never read To Kill a Mockingbird? She took over your class when you were pregnant with Michelle?"

"That was thirty-two years ago."

"Whatever happened to them?"

"He died. We went to his funeral. She moved to Nashville. You open her Christmas card every year."

"That's too bad, I liked them."

She just stares. The guy who originally sang the nominated song in the Disney picture starts singing the nominated song from the war picture instead of the gal who originally sang it. She was onstage earlier singing the nominated song from the sad hereditary illness picture which was originally sung by the guy who comes on in thirty minutes to sing the song from the Disney picture. Glenn does not look impressed with any of these songs, so far. He's more impressed when he hears the sound of his own name, spoken quietly. "Glenn. You always liked George Kaminsky."

"I did, Vick, I really did. But you know, you never can have a real conversation with George. There's no exchange of ideas. I don't know what it is. Maybe we just have nothing in common."

"You prosecuted rapists and murderers together for twenty-five years."

"Believe it or not, Vick, that's not really a solid basis for friendship."

They rest for a while and eat and watch the show. Vicky takes some of Glenn's beer and two or three chips. That guy who wrote the picture about Africa gazes fondly at the Oscar he's just won and apologizes that he doesn't have time to thank anyone except the two dozen individuals and five production companies he's already thanked. A commercial comes on for La-La Cola, that carbonated tequila drink from Baja California that apparently is being guzzled by people grooving to street music all over the world. Glenn starts snapping his finger and pointing at his wife. "There was, there was a couple that we, we looked at slides from our Iceland trip. Didn't we? He had gray hair and she had sort of blonde hair and played the piano?"

"That was your mom and dad, Glenn."

"Oh. You're right. No wonder I liked them." With her eyes closed, his wife is rubbing her temples and doing some deep breathing. "Look, Vick. I'm not very good at coming up with names. You're the one, wull, you know these things better than I do. Just pick a nice couple, anyone, and I'll be more than happy to—"

"The Connors."

Glenn hardly ever stammers. "Those Connors?" he says. His thumb flicks westward toward the TV and wall unit.

"We've shared a property line for three years. Don't you think it's about time?" she says. "We got just a little bit neighborly?"

"Vick, I don't want to get close with my neighbors, not like that, especially if we share a property line. What if we become best friends? We'd never get a moment's—"

"I knew it, I knew you'd never really want to do this. Forget it, Glenn. I know you don't want to. It's okay. I'll just live with it. I'm getting used to that. I'll survive." She takes an apple slice and scoops peanut butter, but the swallows don't seem to make it very far down the pipe, and it's not just the peanut butter. Despair is an effective muffler for stronger vocal chords than Vicky's. "Don't you feel the need to interact with other people?" She says the words but they filter out gurgly.

Glenn's hearing is good, though. If not his listening. "I like being with you," he says. "And the kids. That's all I need. Or want."

"Hon, the kids have their own lives. How often are we gonna see them now that they're both out of state?"

"We'll go visit."

"Sure, but. What about the other fifty weeks of the year? Just live like hermits? I get lonely, Glenn."

The makeup people throw another couple years on Glenn. "Oh." He rubs the stubble under his lips and stares at Ryan's wooden coaster set. A Mother's Day project from Shop class. Then the makeup hardens into a mask of gloom. The mask turns toward the TV. It sees the five Best Actress nominees blushing at the camera and holding their husbands' hands. Their respective husbands, not communal. It sees the winner thunderstruck, fortified with kisses, applauded and spotlighted. Glenn turns toward Vicky and tells her that she's right. They're not going to invite anyone over to watch the Oscars next year.

She says it's okay, she's not expecting anything to change. They're who they are.

"The reason," he says, "that we're not going to have anyone over for the Oscars next year is that you and I are going to be at the Oscars, live and in person. As guests. All right?"

"Super. I'll wear the dress I wore to Michelle's graduation."

"No," he pats her thigh, "you'll get a new dress. This is not a joke."

"Good. Which designer should I represent, Givenchy? Oscar de la Renta? Hair up or down?" After she pushes as much of her short hair as she can to the top of her head, she lets it flop. "Hey, maybe I'll knit myself a dress." She seizes her needles and does a live marionette, knitting in the air in fast-motion. "They've never seen anything like that on the Red Carpet."

"Now you're making fun of me."

"I'm not. Whaddya mean?"

"I really want to do this, Vick."

"Do what?"

"Get you to the Oscars."

"How? Why?"

"Because, of everything. I don't want you to be disappointed."

"I'm not. I'm fine."

"Well, I'm gonna do it."

"How?"

"Get invited."

"By who?"

"I don't know. We've got a whole year."

TWO

Although the guy doesn't stand a snowball's chance in El Centro of winning, Glenn's been saying that he's halfway decided that he might actually think about voting for the guy. To Vicky's horror, when he says it he sounds like he means it. The nomination is up for grabs and Glenn wouldn't mind seeing somebody shake up the system. If anybody can shake it up, and has the money to build a big enough blender, it's Mr. Arthur Trombo, the coal and gas magnate and part-time conservative talk radio host who lives in Trombo Trillium in downtown Pittsburgh. And whom every American either loves or hates, unqualifiedly.

The handy thing is that finally Glenn has the time to keep up with the news, and this year there's actually something worth keeping up on. Since December 29th when he turned in his key to the evidence locker and his official copy of the annotated Penal Code, Glenn's been able to yawn and stretch and say the following whenever he sees his brother-in-law: "The beautiful thing about retirement, Phil, is that I can wake up when I want, go to sleep when I want, eat when I want, drink when I want. And I don't even have to want if I don't want."

When Glenn started calling his wife "Your Honor" and addressing the judge as "Honey", he knew it was time to retire. Thirty-nine years as a trial attorney was enough. Especially in L.A., where Deputy D.A.'s are worked like oxen, under an iron yoke and plowing a rocky land.

Now with his newspapers, his crime novels, his records and tapes, there's a contentment in the old prosecutor that seems to have Vicky puzzled and a little hopeless. She finds moments in her busy schedule to stand and wonder at her husband, as though there's someplace he should be or something he should be doing. And he is dragging his stockinged feet against ever doing it. When she unlocks the front door around 2:45 and finds Stravinsky playing and those stockinged feet swaying, it does not seem to be the apex of her day that Stravinsky might have hoped for.

"Glenn?"

Vicky might not have guessed Stravinsky, she might have guessed Mozart. Sometimes she's a little bit off. Or a lot. A couple of centuries, a Renaissance or two.

Vicky's open purse gets slumped on the dining room table. All the purse wants to do is sit and gape at the violins and cellos. Vicky does not.

Thrown on the kitchen counter, her keys gleam with pride at the trumpets and the French horns. Vicky, towards midafternoon, has developed a dull layer of tarnish.

Heaved upon the parquet flooring, a jumbo pack of toilet paper can settle comfortably. It has a soft spot for oboe solos. Vicky hasn't. Vicky's a little perspiry when she walks into the den.

"How were things at school?" Glenn is smiling. Not quite shouting. And Vicky rolls an invisible knob between thumb and forefinger until he turns down the orchestra and fine-tunes his smile. "How were things at school?" Not quite not quite shouting.

"Fine." Since she's standing between the back of the couch and the credenza, Vicky might as well smooth out the wrinkles in the afghan. She might as well decide to unfold and refold the whole thing, while she's at it.

"Did they have anything for you to do?"

"I shelved books. Showed a couple transfer students how to check materials out. Relieved Bridget for a while at the Reference Desk."

"Why did you leave so early this morning?"

"Aunt Phyllis had a doctor appointment."

"Oh. You had to skip the gym, huh?"

"No, I went. But not very long, I had to go for that smog check."

"Oh yeah."

"Passed."

"Sure, I figured. You didn't have a chance to get over to, uh—"

"Drug Mundo? I got your stuff. Had to get my prescription."

"Oh, that's right. Come sit, Vick. Rest a minute. The Second Movement is coming up." He moves a small stack of illustrated books from the couch to his lap, along with the newspaper that panned the Oscar host for thinking he's funny enough to host the Oscars. "I don't think you've ever heard that part. Have you? It's practically my fifth or sixth favorite movement of all time." Glenn flings his eyebrows at the record cover propped against the wall unit beyond the green carpet. Some of the writing is worn off. You can barely read the word Orchestra. Latvian and National would be anybody's guess.

Vicky is suddenly pensive. She is looking. She is looking pensively at the curious items he just placed on his lap. Or the place where he no longer has a lap because of the fact that he has barely moved a muscle in the past ten weeks. "Glenn," she says pensively, "where'd you get the books?" She swallows pensively.

"The library."

"Any special reason?"

"Just curiosity. Oh, I would have picked up something for ya but I wasn't sure what you had on tap for reading."

She unpockets her phone and displays it. "You could have—" That's as far as she gets. Maybe that's as far as she wants to get. The First Movement sounds like it's wrapping up because the timpani starts pounding. Glenn's perusing one of the books. It's called *Oscar: An Intimate Biography*. It's colorful. It would look nice on their coffee table.

"Hey, did you know that from 1927 to 1986 there were three hundred fifty-two films nominated for Best Picture, and this guy has watched them all?"

Whether Vicky knew that or not doesn't seem to matter to her. As she looks at her husband the thing that seems to matter is that this is not starting out as one of The Best Years of Their Lives.

THREE

Vicky finishes watering all her succulents in the backyard and no sooner sits down a little breathless under the umbrella than her husband joins her. She needs to know, since he's here, what things he's out of if she goes shopping this afternoon. His main concern is dried fruit, since the prunes she bought him three weeks ago are almost gone.

"Wow, that was fast," she says.

"They have potassium," he says. "Besides, you know."

"How's your cereal situation?"

"We're okay, I think."

"Gosh, I came into the kitchen this morning and looked out the window and there was the Red Breasted Grosbeak eating seeds on the tray. A ground squirrel was poking around under the apple tree, and an orange hummingbird came up to the window to say hello."

"You're just a regular Snow White, aren't you, with all your animal friends." He opens his book and finds his place.

"You. With your nose always buried in a book."

"Not just a book. Grisham."

"Aren't you tired of the law yet after forty years of the stuff?"

"Nupe." He is somewhere in the Deep South with a hitman who kicks dogs and shoots little birds while he's waiting for his victim to make a move.

She sighs and watches the little finches and sparrows of her backyard pursuing their flight schedules and nibbling the perfectly good leftover rice from the Chinese restaurant that Glenn wanted to eat but now he won't have a chance.

"Honey," Glenn says. He's back from the lower Mississippi.

"Huh."

"You look really nice."

"I do?"

It's hard for Glenn not to drop his eyes at times like these but he lifts them at the last second and Vicky is always there to record with hers. From the pointy top of one of the cypress trees along the back fence even sharper eyes are recording. A young Red-tailed Hawk sways from a tiny branch sixty feet up. And then is gone.

FOUR

Three weeks is a good time frame for reading a small stack of books, or studying a new subject. Libraries are very generous that way, and you can usually get another three weeks extension if you need it. Glenn doesn't need it. The books are on the passenger seat. Well, one slid off when Glenn made that left turn.

Glenn's in the driver's seat. The car is in the number two lane, westbound, on the main boulevard. It's a Monday. The stores are open but traffic is still light. The sun is behind Glenn and above his rearview mirror. Ahead are low clouds starting to break up. The dew is almost dried off the hood. The classical station is playing something by Edward Elgar. Glenn seems okay with that. While he's at a red light Glenn looks over and the used book store he browses once in a while is gone. Now it's all signs and posters, and some balloons with slogans. Red balloons. The biggest sign says Independents For Trombo Campaign Headquarters. There's a parking space in front for Glenn. The broken meter doesn't do anything to his face. When Glenn walks in there's only one Independent

For Trombo. She wears a Trombo campaign button and baseball cap. Gray pants suit. Maroon sweater vest. Orthotics. She should not be trying to hoist that big coffeemaker by herself.

Glenn helps the lady set up the big coffeemaker and shows her how to work it, since they had the same kind in the break room at the D.A.'s office. Afterward, the lady seems so relieved she lets out one of those little sighs where the voice starts at an upper register. "You're a knight in shining armor, young man," says the lady. That little flirty gleam in her eye is probably not bona fide. Probably glaucoma. Glenn didn't shave this morning. He's serving the coffee while she sits down behind her reception desk and forages for forms and things. "I hope you're here to volunteer."

"Uh, mostly just to find out a little more about the, uh, campaign. Actually, I'm a registered—"

"Shhhh!" says the lady. "That's all right, anybody can join up. They never check."

"But I always vote inde—"

"Shhhh."

"pendently."

"It doesn't matter."

"I see."

Glenn sips coffee and shifts his weight on the metal folding chair. Ten minutes later Glenn is wearing a Trombo teeshirt—just so she can get an idea of the sizing, the lady says—and has learned nothing about the campaign. The lady has learned almost everything about Glenn.

"Wull, I don't know, Virginia, I just never thought I was cut out for politics, I guess. Although I did run for Superior Court Judge once. It's hard to knock out an incumbent judge. Darn near impossible." Glenn yanks the string of one of the red balloons and then releases it to bounce against the ceiling. He's done that about fifty times now.

"Well, Glenn, when Mr. Trombo gets in he'll make sure that talented people like you become judges or governors or whatever they want to be. He's a wonderful man, Mr. Trombo. He's going to bring jobs back to America. He'll fix Social Security. He'll get rid of all the criminals and send them back where they came from. I don't think there's anything he can't do if he puts his mind to it. Don't you think so?"

"All I know, Virginia, is that things are so screwed up—sorry—that we need drastic change."

When Glenn gets back to his car his arms are full of gear, the totality of which he spills into the back seat, to wit: the Trombo teeshirt and matching cap, campaign fliers, bumper stickers such as Raise Profits, Not Taxes, red white and blue America Only beer koozy, an Arthur Trombo Halloween mask with bright red hair and exaggerated widow's peak, two Trombo for America Only yard signs. And contact information for the local organizing committee which would be meeting the third Saturday in April. At a church.

Most of this campaign stuff was generously paid for by the Americans Against Un-Americans or Anyone Who Doesn't Quite Look or Act American Political Action Committee. It says so in the fine print. Right there at the very bottom of those fliers.

FIVE

Glenn seems glad that there are only three other people on the tour and Vicky seems disappointed. It was Glenn's idea to come on a Monday. Glenn seems glad that the three other people are Japanese film students in summer dresses who giggle. Vicky seems tired of waiting for them to get out of her camera shot. But since she's trying to video three hundred sixty degrees and they're clustered around Moesha the tour guide in the middle of the gaping lobby, where can they go?

Moesha plays "Hooray for Hollywood" on her cell phone and dances for her little audience. She's got some moves. But note that she's working as a tour guide. "If you have any questions at any time," she says and switches Benny Goodman off before he can cap his solo, "feel free to raise your hand, I'll do my best to answer them. If I don't know the answer I'll just make something up." She gets giggles, but she's still working as a tour guide. "I'm joking, I'm just—is everyone here familiar with the Academy Awards? The Oscars?" she says to the three film students.

"Oh, yeah, yeah."

"Unfortunately, they don't give me Oscar statues to hand out, you can buy some very nice plastic ones in the gift store." This joke goes over with the Americans. She takes them to the area where the Red Carpet is rolled out a week and a half before the Oscars, she says, covers sixteen thousand five hundred square feet, and undergoes various other logistical operations before and after the Awards. "Any questions on any of this information so far?"

Vicky wraps up her video of where the Red Carpet isn't.

"Do you have a favorite Oscar host of all time?" Moesha says. "My favorite is definitely Ellen DeGeneres, I thought she did a phenomenal job. My second favorite is probably Hugh Jackman, in 2009." Glenn nods like he could have guessed.

"Over here you have the VIP Lounge, called the Dolby Lounge. Step on in, over there you have an actual Oscar." It's encased. Somebody did the lighting.

"Oh it's real?" says the girl with the Hollywood walking tour map.

"This is a real Oscar—"

"Aaaah."

"This was an Oscar, one of twelve, that Dolby won for what we call Technical Achievement, which is—did we lose somebody? Weren't there three of you?" She looks in the lobby. "Here she is." The girl with two cameras runs in out of breath. Moesha says they can take a moment and all belly up to the VIP bar to order imaginary cocktails from an imaginary hot bartender.

"My wife will have a Shirley Temple," Glenn says, "but I don't drink". He says it for Moesha's benefit. Moesha's touching things on her phone. Vicky's heard that one before and looks a little glum taking a video of a place that should have famous people and clinking glasses but doesn't.

"Okay, well while you follow me down this way toward the Theatre itself, I'll ask you if any of you have ever heard the term Seat Fillers before? You have?" Glenn has his hand raised. He's nodding and Vicky's jaw explores an odd angle. "On the night of the Academy Awards we have what we call Seat Fillers. If a celebrity gets up to go to the bathroom or get a drink or snack, they don't want the Theatre to look empty. So, we have two hundred fifty Seat Fillers on the night of the Academy Awards. They are lined up in the hallways and have to rush in and sit next to some celebrity or celebrity's husband or wife until the person gets back."

"Do they get paid?" says Vicky.

"They do not, they are volunteers and they must be an immediate relative to someone who works for ABC Television, or Price Waterhouse the accounting firm. So the best way to get the job is to marry into it." The film students look at each other.

"It sounds kind of stressful," says Vicky.

"It can be. So speaking of stress you are now standing front row and center of the nail-biting capital of the world. This is where the magic all happens on Oscar night. Pick a seat and see how it feels. You might be sitting where Steven Spielberg sat, or Julia Roberts or Whoopie Goldberg." Moesha points out the balconies, the side boxes, the orchestra pit. "This is a huge theatre," she says as they each try out several seats, "nevertheless there are too many Academy members to attend every year. So there's a random lottery. If they attend one year they have to sit out for two years to get back into the lottery."

"One of my mom's cousins was a member of the Academy," says Vicky. "He was a sound editor. Stanley," she says aside to Glenn. He nods. He cranes his head toward the highest balcony.

"Oh, really?" says Moesha. She checks her phone, which says 3:22 pm.

"They used to send him all the films on VHS so he could screen them and vote."

VHS was quite a while back, according to Moesha, then they went to DVD and now it's all downloads. "Folks, any questions about the Theatre, any Hollywood gossip you might want to know?" She gives them a five count. "No? Okay." So she's going to take them around backstage, she says. And they should watch their step going up, these stairs are not well lighted. And right this way. And here they are walking out on stage. And she wants them to imagine what it feels like to the presenters or the winners who look out into this fabled space studded with a galaxy of their fellow stars.

They're all too surprised at being on stage to do any imagining. Glenn tells Moesha that he hasn't prepared his acceptance speech yet.

That's okay," says Moesha, who is prettier than she knows, like a forgotten Hollywood classic. "You can just make it up on the spot. They do that half the time anyway."

"Oh my." Vicky looks up into the rafters. She gives Moesha her phone to take a picture of the two of them on stage with the backdrop of the theater. She puts her arms around Glenn and they pose enwrapped like there are approaching hordes of zombies on the screen. Then she tries to take a panorama video but her phone won't let her, it's full. "Dammit."

Glenn shrugs.

Moesha says they're taking the elevator to the balcony. It's like a hospital elevator. "Okay, here we are. Now in a minute we'll be going left down that hall but first let's go out onto the front of the balcony to get a slightly different view."

"Aaaaah," say the film students to the Dolby Theater. The Dolby Theater yawns back.

"Do you mind if I ask if you're paid for this or is this a volunteer thing?" Vicky turns to him and her eyes widen and narrow at once, which is impossible except where Glenn is concerned. She makes her tongue go tisk.

"No, we're on payroll."

"Are there usually openings, do you know?"

Moesha doesn't know at the present, he'd have to check with Personnel.

"I suppose one of the fringe benefits is you get to attend some of the events. Concerts. Award shows."

She says it's a rotation system. She says it's based on seniority. She's attended several wonderful concerts. She saw the Oscars three years ago. "My turn will probably come up again in about two years."

"You're too young to have been here that many years."

She started as a high school intern, she says and begins ushering them back to the wings.

Glenn nods, a completely innocent curiosity is now satisfied. Vicky almost catches Glenn's eye but such innocence is blind so she snubs the old meddler, she marches after Moesha and the others.

"Any other questions?" She means other questioners. "Now we'll go down the Winners' Walkway. After the Awards finish, this area is screened off to give the winners a moment of privacy." Moesha walks backwards and gestures at curtains. "They can cry, freak out, whatever they need to do." Vicky doesn't seem to appreciate what a sweet and funny piece of Hollywood trivia this is. She is staring straight ahead and one shoulder is pulled in tight, it wants nothing to do with the person it is married to.

"Then at the end of this hall they station a makeup artist to give them a last minute touchup before they go on to the press interviews and after-parties." This dash of glamor that seems charming to Japanese film students does not divert Vicky. She finally turns and looks over her high-minded shoulder.

"Where's my husband?"

They all go back to the balcony. Three private boxes overhang the left side of the orchestra section. In the middle box Glenn stands and looks down at the stage and looks around the huge theatre and shades his eyes with both hands like Geronimo's scouts on a red rock canyon.

"Glenn!"

"Those doors were marked Authorized Entry Only," says Moesha.

"Oh my dear god," says Vicky.

SIX

He thinks the pizza was better in the old days in Parker Center. He takes another slice.

"Maybe," says Ingraham. "Doesn't your wife feed you?" The guy turns what little neck he has to the end of the conference table where empty carryout boxes make stairsteps to heaven.

"It took you guys an eon to figure out what you wanted to do with all this nonsense. I only stayed for the pizza."

These guys are born mimics, they all do outrage. Ingraham's clammy face does it the best. Ingraham's on his second red pepper packet. He adds extra flakes before every bite.

"Come on. Your day was dull and humdrum until this."

"Glenn," says the middle aged guy with the notepad and coffee and arms crossed and no pizza, "tell me you're just a little sadder and wiser from this experience?"

"Sure, Sobel. I'm sad I got arrested for nothing. I'm wiser about the paranoia level in Hollywood, especially tour guides."

Ingraham sucks brown soda from a can and wipes his mustache. "They take security very seriously at those venues, Glenn. You know that."

Glenn swivels his chair and looks out at half-hearted rain, and dusk, and street lights on First Street, and the ghost of City Hall that filters through all of that ambiguity.

"Do you feel any lighter," says Sobel, "like some load was lifted off you? You know? Do you think on some level you were hoping to get caught, Glenn?"

Glenn swivels back. "Do me a favor, don't overanalyze this. Don't make this into a psych thing and start throwing around labels. Passive-Obsessive or whatever the disorder of the day is. I knew you when, Sobel, remember? Before you got your degree and you were working Counterfeit Goods in Koreatown?"

"I think you mean Manic-Aggressive."

"You're not helping, Ingraham," says Sobel.

Pasqual has this smile. He says he thinks Ingraham's diagnosis is incredibly astute. He likes it. He tears open a little packet. Pasqual's smile fights him as he mops a moist towelette around his greasy mouth and beard. "Why don't you go back," he says, "and become a police psychologist. Like Sobel." He'd even hire Ingraham on at the D.A.'s office, he says. They could use a good in-house shrink.

"I—hello?" Ingraham evidently enjoys the first four bars of Chopsticks more than most people. "Why? No. You are? How many shots? Don't you have any other. What? Don't you have any other task force. Who said so? Any other task force detectives who could. Huh? Don't you have anyone else who could. Well, not really. What about Yoshimura? Oh yeah, I forgot he. How soon? Make it forty-five. I know, I know." He disconnects. "Crap," he says. "Off-duty cop fired at a Defrauding an Innkeeper suspect." Sobel and Pasqual shake their heads. Ingraham stands up and puts a hand on Glenn's shoulder. "Look,

Stover, just get involved in something healthy. Golf, archery, anything. Find your passion. Get a dog, maybe."

"I have an allergic wife," he says.

"A giant tortoise?" says Pasqual. "Call her Shelly. Here, Shelly."

"Maybe I shouldn't have retired so soon."

The other three trade looks. "You know what you should do, Stover? Volunteer at one of these nonprofits. I've got a friend who just retired and he gives advice to poor people at a legal services place three times a week. He loves it."

"That's a great idea, Pasqual," says Sobel. "My wife retired and she takes yoga and qigong and she's writing a book. *Blue Goes With Everything: How to Make the Best of being a Cop's Wife.*"

"Let me know when it comes out, will ya?" says Pasqual.

After Ingraham leaves, Sobel turns on the conference room video monitor and gets the Dodger game. "Very therapeutic, baseball," he says. He passes Pasqual the bag of cinnamon curls and the two of them start discussing a trial where the arresting officer has been having night terrors since his brutal cross-examination by the public defender. The cinnamon curls are on the table by Glenn's elbow but he's staring at the video monitor. Dodgers got two on base and Glenn has the face of a Phillies fan.

"You remember that case with the Tilt-A-Whirl operator who raped those girls at the County Fair?" he says, after about nine minutes. The other two guys were in the middle of analyzing Judge Seacrest and the little flask he keeps in the pocket of his robe. "Remember how he might have gotten away if it hadn't been for that lady and her Second Place blueberry pie?"

"Yeah, sure Glenn," says Pasqual. "That was a tough case. You wanted thirty-nine years and the judge gave him six, because the guy claimed that the constant plunging of the rollercoaster cars and screaming riders had given him PTSD."

"Plus the persistent aroma of the kettle corn had overtaxed his impulse control."

"You brought in the Dime Toss lady who said he molested her when she was a minor and was selling snow cones. What a sleazeball."

"Yup," says Glenn, resting his chin on his fist. "That woulda made a great movie."

7

SEVEN

Glenn walks into the room just in time. A very happy lady is waltzing through her front door and into her living room and telling everyone about the newest generation of plugins from Erewhon Air with a feature that allows the busy consumer to activate or adjust their product remotely from their cell phone, so that a perfect fragrance will be awaiting them upon their arrival home after a hard day at the office. Animation flowers are swirling out of the place where the thing is plugged into the wall and all around the lady. The lady is smiling and her lips are not moving but the voice that is talking over the picture seems like it could be the kind of voice that she would have if the writers and the producers had decided to tape it with synchronized sound and if she could dance without getting winded. "Exclusively at Bed, Body and Barrel for $29.99 with $5.00 mail-in rebate, while supplies last. For the discriminating noses in YOUR family." This part just has a snapshot of the product and words and numbers in different sizes of print including rows of tiny ants at the bottom.

Glenn squints at the TV which gives his nose a very discriminating character. "So when do you wanna do it?" he says.

"Anytime." Vicky is looking at her phone and watching a recorded interview of Senator Merrill whom President Brown just endorsed. The famous interviewer is asking her how it would feel to be the first female president if she wins the nomination and the general election, and what she would do for women's rights and gender equality and all the other things that her party cares about more than the other party. Vicky hits pause.

"What shall we fight about?"

"She said make it sort of generic."

"How can you have a generic argument?"

"No specifics, she said nothing that could actually hurt the other person."

"What's the fun in that?"

"Glenn."

"Wull, turn off the TV."

"There. Better?"

"Mmmmh. So you start." He sits down on the couch in his usual place. The cushions sag.

"Why me?"

"I don't know where to start."

"What am I, the wizard of arguments?"

"As a matter of fact—"

"Yes? Go on."

"Let's just forget about it."

"We can't."

"We're grownup adults, we can do what we want."

"We also have issues."

"That's not what I heard."

"Maybe you should try listening sometime."

Glenn's eyebrows go up. He's wise to the game and he shakes a finger. The third shake freezes in air, and if forefingers had a voice this one could be saying Ah, ah, ah in a chess match between rogues. "What's that supposed to mean?" he says.

Glenn's skinny left leg swings up onto the couch so that he can scoot around toward his wife, who reclines Cleopatra-like in her spot. She has callouses on her big toes and the bottoms of her feet. It's time for new nail polish and a pedicure but right now she is smiling and he is smiling and they are the kind of smiles that know each other's worth.

"What do you think it means?"

"I asked you first."

"Yeah, well I asked you last." There's a brown hair of Vickyish length on the shoulder of her pajamas that she plucks and drops on the carpet.

"Well two wrongs don't make a right."

"Don't start throwing platitudes around, that's just like you when you know you're backed into a corner."

"At least I have a corner, you're out in left field."

"Are you gonna start with the baseball metaphors again, I thought we decided to strike those from the conversation."

"Oh I get it. And where was I when this was decided?"

"How should I know, what am I, the reigning Jeopardy champion?"

"Oh that's funny, use humor to avoid the question."

"At least I have a sense of humor."

"As if I don't?"

"I didn't say a thing."

"You never do."

"Well somebody needs to be the listener once in a while."

"So we're back on listening again."

"I never left it."

"Well I never got an answer to my original question."

"What was so original about it?"

"You know what I mean."

"That's just it, I know exactly what you mean."

"Well that's a fine how-do-you-do."

"How-do-you-do to you too."

"Oh that's cute, if you were any cuter you'd be on, on. . . Aaaaaaaaaaaaaaaaagh—"

"Ghaaaaaaaaaaaaaaaaaaa—"

Three minutes. Four. Five. Pillows are strewn. Afghan is a crumpled mass. Vicky is collapsed panting, her bangs plastered to one side and her head cradled between the arm and back of the couch. Glenn is mopping his eyes with his handkerchief and there are high-pitched noises in his throat. One last fit of coughing racks his upper body and whips his head. They are breathless, wiped out like the aftermath of civil war. They each let out a deep vocal sigh.

Glenn picks up a business card sitting next to Vicky's reading glasses on the coffee table. "I've never heard of the Western College of Practical Psychology. What's a PsyD? How long did she say she's been practicing?"

Vicky says she's not sure and that she'll call in the morning and cancel their next appointment.

EIGHT

From a big plastic bag of birdseed she got at the dollar store Vicky puts seed in all her trays and feeders. "Hi, Scrubby," she says to the Scrub Jay squawking above in the apple tree. She knows she's been a bad mommy she tells the dramatic blue flicker of color perched like a sentinel in the small upper branches. She'll put some extra to make up for being late.

She walks away to put her bag down, Scrub Jay descends to his favorite tray and all the little chirpy birds flitter out of hiding to wherever seeds can be found. Her phone rings. "Hi, Honey."

Vicky starts pacing and talking. She is deep in conversation. She paces this way and that. When she paces to the apple tree the little birds flutter up to the branches. When she walks away the little birds come back down to the various feeders. Vicky is oblivious.

"No, Grandma put brown sugar but I use molasses." The little birds fly up into the tree. Scrub Jay doesn't care, he eats until he's full and then flies off to his nest with a mouthful of seeds to go.

"Don't you think you might want to get it X-rayed?" The little birds come back down to their fitful breakfast.

"Honey, Peter isn't thinking of quitting before he has a firm job offer, is he?" The birdies fly up.

"Is she housebroken? That's good. How big is she? Oh my gosh." The birdies fly down.

"—too much time on his hands, I don't know what to do with him anymore." They fly up.

"Yes, he's talking about going to one of their meetings. He doesn't seem to care that the guy is a total jerk." They fly down.

Pacing this way and laughing loud about the irony of life. Up.

Pacing that way and almost crying about the way things were before. Down. Little finches and sparrows are very adaptable and tolerant creatures.

"Bye, Honey. Love you, give our love to Peter." She stops pacing and stands stationary for a moment. She breathes. She looks around. A family of quail is emerging from the bushes, like Munchkins of Oz, peeking out, unsure and fearful, but curious. Vicky creeps in slow motion to one of the lawn chairs. The adult male struts forth, blinking and checking all directions. The pretty female follows and the little, tousled, half-grown chicks tiptoe out after her and in a matter of seconds it is buffet brunch for the quail family.

Vicky watches them, happy, pecking at the seed trays and scratching in the dirt. When faint bumping and banging sounds start to float in from the front yard, Vicky turns her head. She sees Ernesto and his helpers coming around to the backyard at the west end. There's a forest of tall potted succulents between them and their leafblower and their garbage can and their rakes and the quail. Vicky looks at the awkward unaware birds like she wants to gather them all up in her arms and protect them from the big bad men.

Before they go up to bed someone has to close the sliding glass door. Glenn has been raving all week about the movies on TCM, and this night is no exception since they just watched *Pal Joey* and Glenn got to sing along with a lot of good old standards and see Sinatra at his most Sinatraesque and look at Rita Hayworth and Kim Novak in abject awe for two hours and then hear host Ben Mankiewicz sum up the picture and give him interesting Hollywood trivia about the production and the stars. So Glenn says he will close the sliding glass door if Vicky will take his empty cheese and cracker plate to the kitchen when she goes to drop off her teacup and get ice water. When Vicky comes out of the kitchen the light is still on in the family room and Glenn is making sounds, so she investigates.

"It's not closing," he says. He's looking at the sliding glass door and trying to shove it the last half inch but it won't budge. He looks at her. She shares his plight. She tries and can't get it any farther than he did. He looks like Sinatra when Hayworth tells him to fire Novak or pack his bags. They make comments about how old the door is and maybe that kind of thing can't even be fixed or replaced anymore. They have to leave the door like that, a little bit open and not locked, and go up to bed. Glenn's footsteps are heavy going up the stairs. Compared to the guy who watched good movies all week he's much older and strangely subdued. He doesn't read in bed tonight, he just turns halfway on his side and shuts his eyes while Vicky holds her book for a long time without turning a page.

It's cool in the morning, Glenn goes down to look at the thermostat and turn off the hall light. He checks the sliding glass door. He opens it and looks down. The air from outside is brisk, there's early morning traffic and

Scrub Jay is squawking above the empty seed trays. Glenn crouches and pulls a pebble from the end of the sliding door track. He stands up and turns the pebble around in his fingers. It's pink and black all marbled together. It's a nice pebble. Glenn closes the sliding glass door and it closes all the way. He stands for a moment with the sliding door closed tight. Then he opens it. He loosens his bathrobe and cinches it up again. He opens the screen door and goes outside. He puts the little pebble in one of Vicky's planters that she likes to put little pebbles in. Then he goes inside and eats a big breakfast of cereal and leftover spaghetti. He is humming something from *Pal Joey* when Vicky comes downstairs for her coffee.

NINE

There's a *piazza* in the angle formed by the large bookseller and the eateries. There's a fountain in the center of the *piazza*. The tables and chairs are wrought iron. Tuscan pizza fills the air. Colorful *gelatos* cool the lips of couples strolling or children frolicking along the cobblestone alleys. Red tile roofs, hanging flower pots. Music in the soft spring breeze.

Vicky with her phone taking videos of people feeding bread crumbs to the birds. Glenn with his sunglasses and his book on Italian-themed movies. Vicky laughing at a small girl in frills prancing with delight for amused onlookers. Glenn eyeing the savory fare on the tables where families chatter and gossip as they eat. The two of them hand in hand, circling the busy *piazza*. A getaway was just what Glenn and Vicky needed. And now was the time that they really needed it.

They needed a getaway and they got away six minutes and 2.5 miles. If they had gotten away a little earlier in the evening they might not have ended up wandering around or leaning against red bricks between Boulangerie and Sushi Mushi while other people hog all the tables and chairs. None of these other people seem to be in any rush to go back to the places that they got away from. The oldies band is playing Otis Redding, so why would they?

Vicky's smile says plainly that she is at The Piazza on the Boulevard for the ambiance and that tables hold little attraction for her as she makes innocent eye contact with the parties who are showing the best progress at cleaning their disposable plates.

There are no plates, tables, chairs, dogs, people, or horizontal space, according to Glenn's eyes. There are only the immediate flagstones upon which he shifts his weight from time to time and the clouds overhead where orange just became pink to match the tips of his ears.

A white-haired lady with her husband wraps up the other halves of their sandwiches and motions to Vicky to take their table before someone else gets wise. Vicky nudges Glenn and they are table owners, and profuse thankers, in a matter of seconds. Ten minutes later Vicky brings one of those tall metal stands back to the table. The card inserted in the prongs is number 84.

Glenn looks around at all the tables and people. There's a girl in a Cancun Cantina polo shirt with a tray of food wandering among the tables. She has passed through twice already with the same tray of food. She is starting to get a little flushed. "Vick, don't you think one of us should just wait there inside for the food?"

She frowns as she shakes her head. "They'll bring it." When the pizza arrives it is cold because the kid passed through at least twice looking for their number and started getting flushed before he stumbled upon them. Vicky complains about the cold pizza but only Glenn hears the complaint, the kid is long gone, with the metal stand and number. "Canned mushrooms," says Vicky about halfway through her first slice. Glenn hadn't noticed, he says he likes canned mushrooms. The band is playing Santana. Conversation is a bit hampered.

Vicky needs more napkins. Glenn gets up then sits down. "Isn't that the uh—" Glenn's wavy eyebrows are not precision pointers but Vicky knows how they work. She smiles and wonders what they're doing way over here and god how long has it been since they've seen them and Glenn thinks they must have come for the baked cod. "See?" he says. The other couple has baskets of food from Angler's Fish and Chips. They've put down their fillets and are acting a little flustered. They're wiping their mouths and hands. "I think they saw us," says Glenn.

"Let's go say hello."

"Shall we bring our food?"

Vicky thinks they should wait until the people ask them to sit down. She thinks the woman looks good, she kept that weight off. Glenn says he always enjoyed spending time with them.

"Did you?" says Vicky.

"I don't know why," says Glenn.

"Because you had a crush on her."

"No. I mean she's attractive, but not to me."

"He's a very bright guy. You had a lot in common."

"He actually reads books, and he plays the bassoon." Glenn just entered a salad-eating contest against the world. He picks up his plate and bolts the last leaves, sprouts, olives and feta chunks. Vicky tugs at various hems and seams, then checks her lipstick.

"We thought that was you," she says. She reached their table in a trot. She bends from the waist where her hands are.

Glenn gives a last glance back across the *piazza* where their food sits. Little birds have hopped from their umbrella to their chairs. "Hey, strangers," he says.

"Well my goodness," says the woman. Her smile comes so fast, so easy.

"Talk about small worlds," says the man once he's got custody of Glenn's hand. "This is really unexpected."

"What brings you out our way," and Glenn looks like he'd just as soon hear it from the woman as the man.

The man says they like this place and they get over once in a while. Vicky says they like it too, it's one of their favorites. The man says they must be pretty close to here and Glenn says just a couple miles down the street.

"Laura, how are the kids? What's Tracy doing these days?"

Tracy is fine, their son is fine. They've got good jobs, they're in good professions. The girl's engaged to a lawyer. The woman asks about Vicky's kids but doesn't use their actual names.

Glenn talks about retirement, the man talks about his practice. They're both following basketball, enough for Glenn to ask the other couple over one of these nights. "Maybe for the playoffs." Vicky was just telling the woman about Michelle's boyfriend's A.A. degree in Social Science but now she stares at Glenn like he's gone public with an exposé of their love life.

"That'd be great," says the guy. "Just not sure if we'll be in town right at that time."

"Sure, check your calendar. We'll just order in. You know, pizza, sandwiches, nothing fancy. A little white wine." Glenn has no idea of the color that is infusing Vicky's face.

"Why don't you give me your number," says the guy, "and we'll definitely—" Glenn gives them his and Vicky's numbers, asks for theirs, and the guy explains how they're in the middle of changing cell phone carriers and all their numbers will be different. But he'll call Glenn just as soon as that's all squared away. Everybody gets a shake or a kiss.

While Glenn and Vicky walk off their dinner and their excitement, they window shop. The travel agency has a special package deal to Southeast Asia, airfare included. Glenn thinks that's unfair to Californians. "How about Hawaiians?" says Vicky.

When they get to the exclusive boutique that Vicky's never been in she turns her head toward her husband. "Glenn. You can't ask people like them over for pizza and salad."

"What's the matter with pizza and salad?"

"Come on. They're used to a different lifestyle."

"Oh. I shoulda said dinner at Le Capucine."

"Anyway, the point is moot, we'll never hear from them." They go up to the end of the shops, past the luxury cinema where they bring food and wine to your seat during the previews. They come back and sit down in chairs where the band is playing, extra loud because nobody thought to turn down the fountain. Glenn's knees and head like oldies. Like them enough to get out of the chair and do what they're doing, but Vicky won't dance.

"Why not, Vick? Look at all the couples out there. Nobody will care."

"We never dance in public."

"But it'll be fun."

"I don't feel comfortable."

"Nobody cares."

"Uh-uh."

"You hardly have to move. Just shuffle your feet. Sway a little."

She can't wrinkle her nose and shake her head without closing her eyes. Glenn doesn't remark that if she can do all that, dancing to Crocodile Rock should be a snap. He sits back in his chair. He liked Elton John's early stuff better. When the band takes its break they each feel a hand on their shoulder. "You two look so cozy."

They both look around surprised and Vicky tells the friendly lady she's sorry she never thanked her for her holiday card and newsletter. The lady has a gray ponytail and is very sincere and asks about their kids by name and is very interested in their present lives and misses the old days when they would see each other at football games and school events. She says she was about to go into the big bookstore and get some coffee and buy a magazine. Would they like to do that and maybe visit a little more? Vicky says they should probably head for home, she's got some odds and ends she should probably finish up and Glenn has an early dentist appointment in the morning. Glenn points to one of his molars.

"Call me anytime. We'd love to see you."

"We will, Linda. It was great seeing you. Good luck with that shoulder."

There's a stone passageway between the nail spa and the big store with imported stuff from all over. It goes to the parking in the back. Fifteen hundred cars could fit. At the end of the passage Glenn and Vicky can hear the band starting up again. A steel door opens in the back and discharges kitchen noise and light into the alley. A person in an apron comes out and tosses full garbage bags into the dumpster, then goes in and the door slams.

It's a song that Gary Lewis did and Bobby Vinton did and a couple of guys before them and they all grieved about the cold, lonely summer and it's a slow song and Glenn and Vicky are dancing behind the dumpster and if there were words that led to that they had to be whispers. Which is what Vicky uses to ask Glenn if he knows that she doesn't need other people, as long as she has him.

"I know."

"And I don't need to go to the Oscars."

"I just get crazy sometimes." There are kisses that forgive craziness and all types of human tendencies. And sometimes they coincide with song titles.

TEN

He shows up in time for the nightly news with Burt Granville. He heads for the recliner rocker. The vertical blinds are drawn to block the evening sun that still attempts to pierce the sliding glass door. He has a glass of milk and today's mail. Both of them are white. Vicky watches him. "Don't sit on your pants," she says. She just mended that pocket with the hole, the pants are folded and lying where she left them on his chair.

"Why not?"

"It's not good for them."

"What could it possibly do?"

"You'll crush them, Glenn."

"I crush my pants every day, all day. Usually from the inside, but what difference does that make?"

"So sit wherever you want. I give up." He sits on the couch.

The first six minutes of the nightly news are heaped with breaking stories that would alarm a tree sloth. Vicky glances up at Burt Granville and his reporters at the more dramatic moments of the newscast without any reduction of her main occupation, which is to scroll nonstop on her cellphone. Down, down, down she scrolls, sometimes up, but ultimately down, down, down, there is no bottom.

She glances up when the Washington correspondent announces that Governor Kandy has dropped out of the race for President leaving Mr. Trombo as his party's only remaining candidate. She also glances up during the segment about the massive wildfire spurred by record heat, drought and winds near Alberta's oil-sands region. And she gives Burt her full attention when he reads the copy about the disgruntled Texas man who brought a shotgun to his former place of employment, killed himself and a former colleague.

"I hate to complain," says Glenn, "but, so far, it's been a lousy millennium. Think about it." Vicky bobs her head a little, she seems to see his point.

Glenn watches the commercials. One of them has senior citizens carrying their kayak to the lake and playing in a rock oldies band, all in slow motion. "What if I don't WANNA ask my doctor about once-a-week Fleboybin for my loved one's moderate to severe Alzheimer's?" he says. Vicky doesn't look up, she's been listening to this kind of comment for years.

"You know, Vick," he says eyeing her, "because of Fredric March I'll never get Alzheimer's?"

Here's one Vicky's never heard before. She makes a fist out of her scrolling hand and puts it under her chin and eyes him back with infinite patience.

"Because he's one of those actors I can never remember. But I do. See? Every day I have to think of his name. Then I know I'm not senile. Fredric March. See?"

"What happens if one day you can't think of it?"

"Then you shoot me."

If it were Dvorak's Symphony No. 8 surrounding him he would not need to fidget but since it's one hundred and twenty Independents For Trombo chattering in the social hall at Great Awakening Church, Glenn fidgets. He glances once or twice down the row to his right. Virginia maybe could have used a little less rouge but there she is at the end of the row looking sincere, sympathetic and asking people questions about themselves. Virginia wears her Trombo for America Only teeshirt and cap, in proud crimson with matching stretchpants. If all these people went to a USC Homecoming game they would blend in very well and Glenn has a championship grin. He also has his Trombo pennant and his America Only mini-clipboard and pen and his notepad with Trombo's picture at the top of each sheet. That's Trombo's smile. Below his picture on the top sheet is today's date in red ink. That's Glenn's writing. The pennant is on a stick. It's good for twirling between thumbs and fingers before kickoff.

A Chairperson with a podium and a microphone can subdue large groups. It's not even a problem. "Okay it's 7:09 we're gonna get started." The Chairperson chuckles and tells some people standing in the back named Joe and Sandra about the two empty seats up front. She conditions that on whether the folks in the second row will let Joe and Sandra by. "There we go. Well." She smiles at the full house. "This is very gratifying. We'll open our meeting tonight as we always do with a prayer and a pledge. You know, the will of the people upholding the will of God, this is the model of America. This is the authority that created our country, only to do the will of God. That's the authority that enacted our Constitution. The Constitution is there to enact the will of God. Pastor Kline?"

"Let's pray," says Pastor Kline. "Father God, in Jesus name we just want to thank you tonight for gathering us together and for the freedom as a free people to assemble and reflect your will. May the Holy Spirit come down and the fire of God anoint us. We have the mind of Christ. Help us, God, elect those that will represent us and reflect your mind. In the name of Jesus our Lord, Son of God, we thank you. And say Amen. Amen."

The Chairperson brings her son up to lead the Pledge of Allegiance. He's wearing his Scout uniform. He salutes the flag. Most of the audience do their hand over their heart. Some of them are left handed. "Please be seated."

Does anyone have any announcements, she wants to know, before they proceed with regular business. One guy stands up and announces a training session on Saturday on how to become a registered gun owner. "There's a little more to it than you might think," he says. Somebody from the National Gun Federation will be there to offer their expertise. So far, Glenn hasn't taken any notes. He glances down the row at Virginia. She must have taken her cap off at the Pledge of Allegiance.

"Okay, well let's get to the monthly reports. Finance Committee, I think you're up first." The head of the Finance Committee is optimistic that their recent fundraising activities will start to pay off. But they're in pretty good shape for the time being. "We can keep the lights on. Ha ha," she says. "Thanks to a nice check this week from Ridgetop Properties."

The Political Action Coordinator takes the microphone and reports several exciting initiatives in the works. A space has been reserved and handouts created for the upcoming Freedom Fest which will be down in Torrance in May. A voter registration drive is planned for the summer and fall. And, a rally is planned for just before the California Primary and Mr. Trombo has been invited to attend. "We are keeping our fingers crossed that he will say 'Hell, yes.'"

"I am so excited for all these wonderful events," says the Chairperson. "Are you?" She holds the microphone out to the audience like Wayne Newton singing

Danke Schoen. No one will ever know how excited the Independents For Trombo really were, audiences don't ignore microphones, regardless of cause.

"Well now to our distinguished speaker for tonight. This is really special for us. Doctor Sheldon Smith is a practicing orthodontist and clinical professor at Upland University College of Dentistry and on the executive board of the Life and Liberty Alliance. Dr. Smith has become an expert on the inner workings of government, and has personally briefed the Trombo campaign on the serious threats to our freedom that he has helped uncover. We are privileged to have Dr. Smith with us this evening, please welcome him at this time.

"I'll never forget the first time I heard Arthur Trombo speak," begins Dr. Smith. "I was driving through Pennsylvania on my way to the National Conference on Malocclusion and Palatal Expansion, and I was listening to early morning talk radio. I won't tell you how many years ago this was, but let's just say I had a full head of hair at that time." This audience is okay with self-deprecating humor but it's not their brand of choice. "Well, I heard a voice that was almost Nixonian in quality, and I heard that voice explaining why taxes are illegal and why labor unions are illegal and I turned up my radio and within five minutes I was mesmerized like I've never been mesmerized before. That, my friends, was Arthur Trombo speaking *From the Gut*, which was the name of his radio show back then. And that, for me, was the moment that crystalized a lot of confused and conflicting ideas I had about politics and our society. I never forgot Arthur Trombo and when he announced last year that he was running for President I knew that that would go down as one of the great days in modern American history." The audience isn't sure if this is the kind of speech that you have to applaud when there's a dramatic line or it's just a heart-to-heart talk. They sneak little looks at their neighbors, nobody tries to clap.

Everybody sits back content and ready to open their hearts. Glenn has written the words "From the Gut" on his notepad. Twice he had to knock the pen on the pad to keep the ink flowing.

Dr. Smith sketches a brief biography of Trombo. His religious upbringing. How the coal and gas magnate's industrial empire began and grew. How the great man practiced and preached in perfect symmetry according to capitalist principles. The manifest destiny of it all. What does Trombo stand for? Dr. Smith reads off that shopping list in plain underlined words. No one else has the vision and the fortitude to accomplish these things. No one else understands what's at stake. "If we get Trombo in the White House and a majority in Congress, they can work for the only thing that can save this country from financial ruin and from socialism: the complete elimination of most federal agencies and substantial reduction of the few agencies that serve a legitimate purpose." Dr. Smith pauses a moment to let the audience swish that around in their mouths. "Why in god's name do we need a Department of the Interior? Hmmmh? A Department of Labor? Health and Human Services, Department of Energy, EPA? But the first one to get the axe: the IRS. And no more raises for federal employees and federal pensioners."

"What about all these drug dealers over at the DEA?" Glenn can't see the person who calls out the question but it's a voice that could be an understudy for several of the Muppets.

"We're going to fire and prosecute these people." There is no hesitation in Dr. Smith's voice.

Glenn takes off his jacket. He rubs the back of his neck. A woman raises her hand. "What about state and local government?"

"Same thing. Full of decay. Abscess. They suck up our tax money and most of it they spit down the drain.

We need to elect Trombo people on the state and local level, too."

Someone else wonders, "How about things like police and fire?"

Of course they need essential services. Dr. Smith is crystal clear about that. But even those have a lot of overbite. "We need strong wires around government. You don't want it growing. It invariably grows crooked. Remember Mr. Trombo's beautiful manifesto that I read you, what was one of the first things? Get rid of all the crooked liberal judges, who are on the take from the civil liberties lawyers. Then we'll get rid of the lawyers. The courts cost hundreds of millions and most of it just goes into lawyers' pockets."

Glenn sighs and looks at the speaker and looks at the rows of people around him. He clicks his pen closed. He fastens it to the little clipboard.

"Friends," Dr. Smith goes on, his moustache tickling the microphone and something more clinical and confidential in his manner, "here's what we're really looking at. Many of you know, and those of you who don't may have had certain suspicions, that there's something rotten below the surface. Under the veneer of our government lies something sinister. I only learned of this deep infection last year. But I am here to tell you that it is real and it is everywhere throughout our government and if we don't do something now to stop it it will only spread. I'm talking about the Bureaucracy Beneath." Dr. Smith explains the whole design perfectly. More than any audience has wanted to know something, this audience wants to know. The Bureaucracy Beneath is a vast network of government employees who were recruited by the BB and who each have a tiny pellet which is actually an electrode implanted in their brain and which is controlled from a central command somewhere in northern Michigan. All of that is a given. But it's more complicated than that. The BB in turn is run by the Philosemitic Cartel of Scientists and NGO's, the Communists, and the Hollywood elite. "How did these shadowy entities get so rich and so powerful", Dr. Smith asks of the magnetic supercharged air in the room. The atmosphere seems to send little stimulating impulses through him. The audience wants to know but they're not sure they want to hear anything that will keep them up during the night. "Hmmmh? What's the source of their worldwide funding? They make billions through their abortion and baby-stealing rings, AND they get a cut from the Chinese government for every dollar of every product sold to America. Can you imagine?"

"Dr. Smith," says the Chairperson, who might have back problems or just likes wandering around the stage while other people talk and who leans in to the microphone for a moment, "the members might wonder why they don't hear about any of this from the media."

"No you won't hear about this from Big Media," says Dr. Smith who seems delighted by her question. "And don't expect to see it in your local papers either. Because the media, with one or two exceptions, are controlled by all of the above. Everything they print or broadcast is filtered through the powers that be."

People are raising their hands. Glenn is shifting his weight on the hard folding chair. His pennant is under his feet. You can just see the "ombo".

"I heard that they put hidden messages in certain TV commercials for nonalcoholic beer," says a woman with one hand up and the other hand on her lap holding a tote bag from that cosmetic company that turned out to be a pyramid scheme.

"No, those are our messages," Dr. Smith says.

"Oh," says the woman.

"You have to know the code. The code is in commercials for baby food."

A guy who sounds like he might want to work in radio says that Angela Merkel is a KGB agent and we should get out of NATO because it's been almost a hundred percent infiltrated by the KGB. He adds a couple more disturbing things about cyber-espionage, kosher gelatin, and the ozone layer. He uses terms like "asset", "black bag" and "microdot".

"Friends," says Dr. Smith looking at the whole audience and not so much at the guy, "the bottom line is that Arthur Trombo is the only man with the guts and the will to expose this evil network and yank it out by the roots. He's the only candidate we can trust because he has absolutely no experience in government."

There's a look on Glenn's face. There is something determined in Glenn's head and shoulders that hasn't been there since the last time he was in jury trial and opposing counsel asked a highly prejudicial question she knew better than to ask. He starts to stand up with his hand raised and his mouth open.

"Excuse me." Glenn looks behind him and to the left. That wasn't his voice. "I don't know who started this, but I work for the government and I can assure you that none of this is true." The young man wears glasses and has a slight Chicago accent. He is standing and slowly straightening, stiff apparently after an hour of sitting. Glenn blinks a few times in the young man's direction, then glances at his immediate neighbors and settles back into his chair. "Somebody is just using you people to spread their ridiculous conspiracy theories."

"Who are you, please, and are you a member of this group?"

"My name is Ron and I don't belong to any group. I just don't like to see disinformation put out there. The stuff you're peddling is dangerous and can hurt people."

"Well, Ron, thank you for speaking up." The Chairperson has taken over the microphone and the podium and is smiling. "That's what freedom of speech is all about. But disinformation is a two-way street. If you work for the government, and if our information is correct, then how do we know you're not one of them. How do we know you're not the one peddling conspiracy theories about us."

"There's no them, Ma'am."

"Well, Ron, this is a democracy. Shall we put it to a vote? Shall we see how many people in this room agree with you and how many agree with myself and Dr. Smith?"

"How can they vote on something if all they know is the ridiculous stuff you've told them? It's just peer pressure."

"Well, Ron, if you're so uncomfortable with the way we do things here, then this is probably not the place for you."

The young man sighs heavily and looks around. Every eye in the place has him in its crosshairs. He moves to the aisle and toward the exit. He turns around. "Read a newspaper, for god's sake. The L.A. papers are not exactly liberal." He goes out the door but his voice carries back. It's saying goodnight to the security guard in the lobby.

There are grades of smugness and the Chairperson's smugness as she returns the microphone to Dr. Smith is a superior grade, by any standard. Too smug to care about a retired guy in the middle, shuffling and excusing himself down his row. "Hello," he whispers when he gets into the aisle.

"Oh you're the nice man who came to the office and we had coffee together. I'm so glad you came." Virginia pulls on the Trombo For President button on her sweater and raises happy eyebrows at the identical one on Glenn's jacket.

"You signed me up," he says. He crouches by her chair.

"Isn't this a wonderful talk. So illuminating."

"I forget your name, but come with me. You don't wanna be here."

Apparently she does. And she is "one of them", even though Glenn is trying to convince her quickly and quietly without causing a commotion that she's not and that deep down she knows this is wacko stuff. When Glenn walks out thirty seconds afterwards he walks out alone but with a shrug.

Later this evening it is proven empirically that two **TROMBO FOR AMERICA ONLY** yard signs fit comfortably in a standard blue trash bin if it's only been a day or two since trash day.

ELEVEN

The world is exploding in the dark, everything is falling into nothingness, there is death and destruction in every direction. Ear-splitting sounds, flashes of chaos. Blinding, crashing, agony.

And then the feature begins. The volume returns to normal. There are opening theme music and credits. It is tranquil, peaceful, civil and orderly. Glenn uncovers his ears and whispers something about the previews being approved for All Audiences and there oughta be a law against it. Vicky whispers that all those movies looked horrible. The feature is a Romanian film with subtitles about a man whose brother died and made him guardian of his three Roma children that nobody knew he had. It is rated PG-13 for some profanity and references to sex. It's a sweet story, but sad, and when the matinee is over Vicky doesn't want to move until the closing credits are done. Glenn listens to the orchestra music and rolls up their empty bag of Peddler Pete's organic popcorn popped with sesame oil that Vicky sneaked in in her handbag.

They walk over to the other side of the mall to the gourmet burger place with loud '50's music and high prices but it's the place they used to take the kids on weekends and sometimes they still get their favorite table.

"I don't like to see a movie the first night it opens," Glenn says. They're in a small booth for two with their menus and ice water.

Vicky is biting the lemon she just squeezed into her glass. She looks up from the senior's menu and pushes her reading glasses tight against her face so that Glenn won't mistake the disdainful glance there.

"You know, opening night jitters and all."

Vicky frowns.

"I like to give them a few nights to settle down. Then I'll see it."

"Droll. Very droll."

While they're ordering, a large group comes in and takes the long table in their corner of the restaurant. It seems to be an extended family group with a few out-of-towners. They're loud but not louder than they need to be to have a large family dinner in a restaurant with bad acoustics. They know what they want and they order family style.

All during dinner the Stovers are like any old married couple and the large family is like any large family gathering: warm, jolly, joking, catching-up. The Stovers don't need much conversation to go with their food, they can eavesdrop and smile at each other sometimes and appear lost in thought.

The Stovers are slow eaters. The family came hungry. Both parties are finished and ready to leave about the same time. The big family gets up and starts saying their goodbyes. The Stovers get up and watch the big family. Glenn and Vicky have these looks on their faces. For a moment it looks like Glenn and Vicky might almost turn to the family and start hugging them and saying their goodbyes. What really is the difference between knowing somebody for thirty minutes or thirty years?

Backpacks now outnumber briefcases. In eight out of ten county government centers backpacks predominate. *Civic Lifestyles*, that glossy magazine on the free rack at supermarkets, did a study. The hands-free aspect was the number one factor. This government center is one of the other two, apparently. Here, people who point usually only have one free hand to do it with.

"That's not Glenn Stover?" With the sunlight rebounding off the lily pond and the fountain and the surrounding concrete mall, some questions require prescription sunglasses.

"I've never seen him in street clothes."

"He might have put on a couple pounds."

"Lucky bastard. Jesus, my wife would go nuts with me around thirty-four hours a day."

"You mean twenty-four."

"Not at my house."

"Cute. Well, she's got him out running errands, it looks like."

"I could handle that part. Sleep til 8, run a couple errands, drink coffee, go back to bed. Beats working for a living. Shoot, it's 8:15 or something, Mark, why didn't you tell me? I gotta hustle, I got court in like fifteen minutes."

"I'll see ya later, Javier, I'm gonna stop and get some—" Javier's briefcase adds more momentum than drag. He is twenty yards away at the employee entrance with his ID out. "—gum."

Glenn's briefcase *emeritus* didn't make the trip. Only a manilla envelope. It's got Scotch tape reinforcement on the flap. It's got headshots inside. It's got enough postage for twice its weight. Glenn cradles it under his arm. In the Post Office, Glenn checks the chute up to his elbow to make sure the package descended.

"Glenn?" For a second his forearm is wedged.

"Heidi?"

Since Heidi is six foot four and has red hair, he probably meant that rhetorically.

"How are you? How's retirement?" She's not looking for answers either. "What brings you out so early, a gentleman of leisure like yourself?"

He rubs his arm. "The chance of seeing you?"

"Well, you found me. You look so rested. How are you spending your time?"

"Cleaning my garage. That should take me through to October." Heidi thinks that's funny but she hasn't seen Glenn's garage. "How are things in the office?"

Things don't sound too choice. Heidi apparently cultivates one of the juicier clusters on the D.A. grapevine. But according to Glenn's face things sound just divine. The more Heidi goes on about burgeoning caseloads and lagging resources, about office scandals and judicial meltdowns, the more Glenn's eyes wander off to some far-flung heaven that they know they will never again actually see.

Glenn passes the lily pond on the way back to his car. The breeze is high but the fountain is low. He only gets sprayed a little.

"Excuse me, where do I go to fight a ticket?" If there ever was a kid who looks guilty of bad driving, it's this kid.

"What kind of ticket?"

"Does it make a difference?"

"Well why do you want to fight it?"

"I didn't do it."

"Do what?"

"Not stop at a stop sign."

"So why did you get a ticket?"

"Quotas. I guess."

"Uh-uh. No such thing. Not since neighborhood policing came in."

"Are you a cop?" Glenn shakes his head and bunches his lip the way cops did before neighborhood policing came in. "A lawyer?"

"Used to work in that courthouse."

"So you could tell me where to go to fight this ticket."

"What do you mean you didn't do it?"

"I stopped. I mean, he says I barely slowed down and I turned the corner at a high rate of speed. There was no way he could see that, it was dark and the street light was out."

"Where was he?"

"No idea. Hiding somewhere, on a motorcycle. He didn't show up til I was halfway down the—"

"Any witnesses?"

"My mom."

"Your mom was with you?"

"No, but she knows that street light was out, and she knows I always stop at that stop sign."

"OK. This is what you do." For the next twenty minutes the kid gets detailed instructions on posting bond, getting a court date, preparing witnesses and exhibits, giving opening statements, cross-examining the officer, testifying in rebuttal, and closing argument. He asks Glenn if he could be his lawyer, since he already basically is. Free, he doesn't have any money.

"I can't. I'm retired."

"Couldn't you still be retired and take my case?"

"No, I'm totally retired. Just do what we talked about and you've got a shot. Tell the truth. You'll be under oath."

The kid thanks him and shakes his hand and Glenn watches til the kid disappears into the courthouse. Glenn turns to go and there is a gentleman standing in front of him and smiling. He looks a lot more retired than Glenn.

He's holding some of the salmon-colored forms that Small Claims Court uses. The forms are trembling and it's not that breezy. "Good morning," says the gentleman. "I wonder if you could take a look at these forms and see if I've filled them out correctly." He turns the papers toward Glenn and points at the section where you describe how much money the defendant owes you, why he or she owes it, and how you arrived at that amount, in about a half inch of space. If Vicky were here she'd have her reading glasses on.

"I'm sorry," says Glenn, "I really don't know anything about civil litigation. I'm sure the clerk at the Small Claims window would—"

"No, I only want to be sure it makes sense to you, as a lawyer."

"How did you know I'm a lawyer?"

"Aren't you?"

Glenn's eyebrows make pink corrugated leather out of his forehead. He blows out air and steadies the free end of the gentleman's papers and reads. "You're suing your insurance company? A tree fell on your garage?"

It was the last Santa Ana, it was an old eucalyptus, and it's a young insurance company that allegedly likes to wiggle out of things. Glenn does a quick editing job and sends the grateful fellow on his way.

"Hello. Am I the next?" This is a young woman with a middle-eastern accent. Glenn has to tell her she's in the wrong place: the immigration department is downtown. While he's telling her two more people line up behind her. While he's consulting with those two, the line grows by three more. Glenn looks down the line and flushes, the flush of a sudden sweat. Some have simple questions. Some just want directions. Some have problems that have no connection to law, government, or even social work. Some need the police. Some need a high-priced law firm. Some need a doctor. Most need money. The line grows, shrinks, grows, and finally, about the time the jury pool gets its mid-morning break, Glenn runs out of clients. He rubs the back of his neck and removes his jacket. When he walks to his car it's with stiff joints and the face of Rocky after the big fight. Minus the open wounds.

The next morning Glenn arrives at the lily pond and this time with his briefcase and water bottle and some string cheese in his jacket pocket. Nonchalant seems to be the look that Glenn is going for, and he does a poor job of going for it. People walk by oblivious. He tries to make eye contact without making eye contact. Collectively, these people are not interested. Individually they seem competent, well-prepared, well-organized, well-represented, well-oriented, well-equipped, and in no need of a lily pond lawyer. Glenn mans his post. He looks down sometimes to see where he went or if he forgot to put on something that morning that people usually put on before they leave the house. The Weather Service's next Santa Ana starts to whip up and people hug their papers and purses and tilt into the wind as they pass him by.

Goldfish love to make eye contact. They don't mind if string cheese sits out unrefrigerated for the two hours that it takes to drain all the promise out of a rosy morning.

It was fog, turning to mist, turning to light drizzle, turning to mist, turning to low clouds, turning to clearing skies, turning to high clouds and smoggy haze. How do L.A. weather reporters weather the gripping drama of their mornings? Are they blown over by these atmospheric upheavals? Or do they revel and splash, looking about them in all directions and chirping, like Vicky's little birdies?

Weather aside, she is always happy to see him come and sit down with his cup of tea under the backyard umbrella. She is not always happy to see him come and sit down with his cup of tea wearing those shorts. She reminds him that he was supposed to have given that pair away a year ago.

"I like them."

"They don't look good."

"You bought them for me."

"That was before your legs got so bony."

"I can't help it."

"David Beckham can wear shorts like that. Not Glenn Stover."

That makes Glenn's eyebrows go up almost a centimeter. Two seconds later he starts nodding. "Married thirty-five years," he says with his free hand upturned, "and now I find out for the first time what my wife really thinks, about my legs."

So because he doesn't have the legs of a world-class athlete they're not fit for human sight. Is that what she's saying? Either he suffers in long pants all summer or he gives up hiking, tennis and cycling? The face he gives her is one of those martyrs in some old painting in a museum.

"When was the last time you cycled?"

"And what about the other 99.99 percent of the human race with their sub-Beckham legs? Are they all guilty of public indecency?"

"Stop."

"Maybe I have to stop wearing short sleeves because my arms don't measure up to Sylvester Stallone's."

"Cheee," she says.

"I'm certainly no Denzel Washington so I guess I better put a bag over my head next time I go to the supermarket. Honey, at my age just be glad I still have my teeth and I can leave the house without a walker. After all, I'm married to the prettiest girl in town. As long as you're right there with me, nobody's gonna be looking at MY legs, you can bet your last—what's the matter, you don't look so good."

"I've been dizzy."

"Since when?"

She shrugs and stares. A Tufted Titmouse zips down to the trays and zips away with a little seed left over from yesterday. He flits to a branch where he can crunch his little snack in safety.

"You got something in your ear?"

She shrugs again. "I'm kind of nauseous."

"You want something? To eat?"

She shakes her head. "Can you feed the birds and water the plants?"

"Oh."

"And we need to sweep the cobwebs around the windows and put those things away in the garage."

He doesn't say anything, just sips slowly from his teacup.

"I was hoping to clean the upstairs bathrooms today," she says.

He doesn't ask any questions such as why all these things suddenly need doing just when she's temporarily out of commission. He doesn't make any comments to the effect that she's not permanently disabled and she'll be fine in a day or two. He sips his tea and watches a lizard on the patio. The lizard nabs a fly with her long tongue and swallows and smiles. Glenn looks at the lizard as if that was his special fly that she swallowed and now what is he supposed to do for lunch?

"Nothing like a nice relaxing cup of tea." He stands up. "I'm gonna give you a kiss, Sweetheart, and then go inside and go to the bathroom." The kiss is on Vicky's pale right temple.

Twenty minutes later he comes back out and sits down. She hasn't moved, her nose is wrinkled up against the world in general. Scrub Jay squawks in the oleander.

"I'm sorry, Honey, I just don't feel too great."

Glenn nods, he knows.

"But could you at least do a little shopping? We really need some bananas. And some cottage cheese. But put on long pants."

TWELVE

The fans cheer and whistle and look very happy and it doesn't seem to have anything to do with the fact that they are beautiful. Being roped off, bottled up, and bundled up when it's not bundling weather and watching other people even more beautiful going arm in arm up a ramp into an air conditioned building seems to agree with them. There is something electric about this crowd, looped together and switched on like holiday lights. Some of them are looking through their cameras or aiming phones but they are of one voltage and one volition.

When Glenn stops walking Vicky stops walking. She holds his arm and smiles. They make an elegant couple. She whispers something in his ear, Glenn nods.

"Madison LeGuin," says the guy with the microphone at the top of the ramp, "how excited are you to be here and be nominated for your first major role in a feature film?"

"I am beyond excited, this is a dream come true, I'm afraid I'm going to wake up and none of this is real."

"Oh, it's definitely real. Isn't it, people?" That's a yes from the people. "And, you are absolutely breathtaking in your stunning gown, tell us about it."

"This is a Maurice Patrice. It's made of taffeta and polystyrene. The color is Amethyst. There are over two hundred feet of hand-stitched embroidery on the skirt and bustle-back."

Glenn looks like there's something funny about the term bustle-back and mouths it at Vicky. He looks around to see if anyone is behind them.

"And now tell us about your gorgeous date."

"Well, this is my baby brother, Tyler. Tyler's on spring break from his school in North Carolina."

"South Carolina," says Tyler leaning a little toward the microphone.

"Well that's gotta be the sweetest thing we've heard tonight on the red carpet. I would love to have a selfie with Madison LeGuin and her baby brother." He puts his microphone in his other hand and gets in the middle and holds his phone at arm's length. While they smile and take pictures the crowd smiles and takes pictures of them taking pictures. Vicky smiles and tries to take pictures but Glenn makes her put her phone away.

"Who's this?" says the red carpet reporter. There's another head in the frame between him and the young actress. "Olivia Cantrell? Did you just photo-bomb your chief rival for Best Supporting?"

"Would I do something so desperate and tacky, Cosmo?"

"You would and you have, Olivia, in every event you've ever attended. What's that in your hand?"

"This? Oops. Sorry, Madison, I forgot I was holding this pineapple margarita."

"Oh no, Olivia," the reporter says as everyone gasps, "you've gone totally berserk this time. Her gown is ruined."

Glenn looks at his elbow. Vicky is squeezing it.

"You did that on purpose." Madison punches Olivia in the gut and the older actress strikes back with a plunging tackle. The fans are screaming. Somebody is going to get hurt.

"CUT." Everyone slackens, everybody looks around expressionless. When colonels shout "At ease" at drilling regiments they get that effect. Beautiful people have two seconds to stare or travel somewhere inward and personal. "Back to one."

Glenn straps an arm around Vicky. They steer their way through assistant camera operators adjusting their lenses, boom operators shifting their equipment and resting their biceps, lamp operators squinting upward and dabbing fingers at glowing metal surfaces, through propmasters and hair and make-up artists, through wiry production assistants and script supervisors, through surprisingly calm production coordinators, through actors trying to find their original marks and remember which line goes with which mark.

"For your next project," Glenn says. He sticks a business card in the hand of the Assistant Director who yelled "CUT". The guy looks at his hand but mostly looks at the rear view of Glenn and Vicky because Glenn and Vicky don't seem to care who they leave gaping in wonder as they continue trespassing through the set.

"What was that?" says Vicky.

"A card."

"What kind of card?"

"What does that street sign say?"

She squints. "*Saddle Sores* Avenue and *Oh That Harriet* Way. What kind of card?"

He puts one in the window of a fake beauty salon. "Aren't we supposed to take a right?"

Vicky takes the card from the window sill and looks at it. The upper left corner has a logo of a judge's gavel. The card says "Glenn R. Stover, Retired Senior Deputy

District Attorney". Then it says "Technical Consultant, Courtroom Scenes and Criminal Procedure". Then it says his cell phone number and his email. "You think anybody's gonna see this?"

He turns his palms and his eyebrows toward the blue Burbank sky. "I've got five hundred of them." Vicky gives him the card and he puts it back in the window. He looks at himself in the glass.

He sticks one on a gaslight in Old New York Street. In Tortilla Plaza he tapes one on the stucco wall of the cantina, right below the poster about a bullfight. In Midville Square he walks up the courthouse steps. He stops and looks. Prosecutions must be down in Midville. He leaves a small stack of cards on the bottom step.

"You know, Glenn," Vicky says, "all of this is fine, if you want to do it. But you know it won't pay off in Oscar tickets."

"I know. We're just here to have fun." He wedges a card into a crack in the hitching post in front of the Buffalo Junction Sheriff's Office. He looks up and down the deserted dirt street and covers Vicky with his loaded index finger while she peers into the Sidewinder Saloon. The Stellar Studios water tower is a Southern California landmark. It rises above them in the background.

"Look where we are," she says passing the *Dads Will Be Dads* house. They both gaze at the homey façade with reminiscing eyes. There's no mail in the homey mailbox at the homey curb but Glenn props one of his cards under the lid.

They reach the corner of *Days of Our Hospital* Drive and *Murder Ain't Pretty* Boulevard. It's a quiet intersection. They go right and in bright sunlight there's Stage 39 and besides catering people and wardrobe racks on wheels and film equipment unloading and construction materials reloading there is a swarm of extras who got there long before the Stovers. Many are lined up at an entrance across the studio street from

Stage 39. You can tell these people are extras because they are dressed in business casual and have luggage. Vicky and Glenn look at all the duffel bags and backpacks and rolling suitcases and then look at the credit union tote bag that Vicky is carrying.

They get in line behind an elderly gentleman and ask him if this is the line for extras and he's probably done some real acting because not everyone can deliver a "Yes" with so many diverging emotions. "It's just us peons," he says. Glenn shifts his weight a few times and sways on his feet and glances around and the old man turns away in little refined shuffles.

Vicky is checking the potted plants that flank the entrance to see if they're real. She thinks they are. She pulls off a few dead leaves. The security guard sitting there watches her. Her uniform is fresh from the dry cleaners. It's shady on this side of the street.

When they get inside to the check-in table a girl wearing an Extra Extra Casting ID badge finds their names on her list. "Husband and wife?" she says.

"Can you keep us together?" says Glenn.

"I can't. Maybe the production people can."

They take their blank vouchers and follow the general flow to the Holding Area. It's marked "Holding Area" and Glenn rolls his lower lip inside out and nods his head in several directions. The room is big and windowless and studded with moving mouths so if someone had been wearing earplugs for an hour and now took them out there would be a blank and alien expression on that someone's face for at least a minute.

The seats are in long rows with a center aisle. The majority are taken but Vicky finds them two together in the middle and they settle themselves and glance around at all the interesting people who are doing what they're doing.

"I remember you now," says a guy sitting in front of them. "We had each other's vouchers once."

"Tim Terry show?" says the guy sitting next to him. He is sipping coffee from styrofoam and hiding the cup under his jacket between sips.

"That was it. I'm Don Flack and you're Dan Flake or something."

"Yeah. That's right."

Glenn asks Vicky for a pen. It's at the bottom of her tote bag. Also his book. He starts filling out his voucher. He gets name and Social Security number. It's going through to the second and third copies. Glenn checked to make sure after "Glenn".

There's a loud sharp voice from the front of the room. "Okay, I need the first three rows to go immediately to Wardrobe to try on gloves. I hope none of you are allergic to Burmese Pythons." A young person with green hair and sleeveless arms and tattoos sits on the edge of the desk and smiles. "Just kidding. I'm Sierra, I'm your 2nd AD and I will be your nanny for the next eight to ten hours." She looks at her watch. It's thick and black with a lot of knobs. She has wrists the size of Vicky's shoulder. The watch could have its own time zone. "Yeah, eight to ten. The good news is we only have seven and a half pages to shoot today." She holds up a rumpled little script. "So, it's a piece of cake, we might have you out early, for those of you who would like to watch the Lakers demolish the Spurs tonight." The Stovers look at each other.

"Okay, who's ready to have fun today? Oh hell, yeah. First of all, is there anyone who hasn't checked in and gotten their voucher? If you haven't, go to the check-in desk. Out that door and to the right. You can leave your stuff here. This is home base, folks, for the rest of the day. When you're needed on set, leave your stuff here. Just don't leave valuables lying around. Now, a few reminders, most of you know these things but it doesn't hurt to hear them again. While you're on set there is no talking. I need you to listen, we will be giving you many instructions and we'll need quiet to be able to do our jobs. If you have a question or there's a problem on set raise your hand. We will get to you when we can. All right? When you're on set turn your phones off. No pictures or videos of any kind, that's the quickest way to get escorted to the main gate of the studio and told don't bother coming back." Vicky takes a deep breath. Her eyes float toward the ceiling lights, possibly imagining tiny body cameras and obscure places on the body that a person could stick them.

"Don't ask for a bigger role or lines. Don't ask for parts in other films, etcetera. Never initiate contact with the actors. Don't even make eye contact. They may be getting into character or chilling out, they don't need you guys distracting them. Okay, any questions?"

Somebody in the front has one. The Stovers and everybody in the back have to cup a hand behind an ear and infer. "No, please wait til you're called," the 2nd AD says. "Everybody's going to be seen by Wardrobe, Hair and Makeup. We will send you by the roles you've been assigned. Be patient, just wait 'til we call you. If you have to leave the holding area to use the restroom, please let me or my colleagues know. You guys have been great. This is gonna rock."

The lady sitting next to Vicky asks her if she's done this before and they find out they're both first-timers and Vicky has to explain to the lady some of the things the 2nd AD just told them and also what a Spectator does in a courtroom scene. The lady looks relieved and shows Vicky pictures of her cats on her phone.

In the seat next to Glenn the young woman looks like she's hoping to stand in for Vivica Fox. Only Vivica Fox isn't in this show. The young woman is doing stuff on her phone that looks important because of the quantum of energy that her fingertips are releasing. Glenn just seems to think that there is irony in the atmosphere of the Holding Area.

"I should have brought something by Tolstoy," he says. He says it for the young woman's benefit and smiles over his shoulder, the one nearest to her. Glenn's lap has a Tom Clancy paperback. His smile doesn't last very long. He has to swallow. She hasn't stopped doing stuff on her phone. Her ears look fine. They don't have anything in them.

In a little while Glenn makes Vicky come with him to the front of the room. The 2nd AD is sitting there playing with her phone. Glenn waits until she says "What's up?" The little ring through her right nostril looks nice when she smiles and her nose widens.

"Sierra, we're both Spectators. We were wondering if we could sit together in the scene."

"You married?" she says. "What's your last name?"

She finds Stover on her sheet of names. "Hey, could we use an older couple dancing or anything?"

"No, we're not really dancers, we just—"

"I know there's no dancing in the script but—" She's looking straight at him.

"Oh, you were—" Glenn points to the little ear device she is wearing. She keeps looking at Glenn and then she says something about where Wang Wei is and then she just looks for a few seconds and then she says something about where Tariq is and where he's supposed to be and then she just looks for a few more seconds and then she just chuckles.

"I'll see what I can do," she says.

Glenn is watching her. She's just looking at him. "Oh," he finally says. "You're talking to me? Thank you." Vicky takes Glenn back to their seats.

About 9:15 Sierra starts sending everyone in waves to Wardrobe and Hair and Makeup. Jurors first. Then Random Court Staff, then Members of the Press, then Spectators. "You all look perfect but we just need you to check in with them so they can bless you. That way they can keep their jobs." Some of the Jurors appreciate wry humor. "Oh, if you have visible tattoos I want you in the front of the line because it's gonna take time to cover those." Everybody looks at their arms, even those who have never had a tattoo in their life.

At Wardrobe Vicky is fine the way she is and Glenn has to put on a v-neck sweater that is brown with a little bit of orange. The head Wardrobe lady tells them how cute they are being married and being extras together. Then they go to the line for Hair and Makeup.

"You a regular?" says the guy in front of Glenn. The back of his neck is hairy but the front has razor burn.

"No, I—"

"Huh?"

"Not a regular. How about—"

"Huh?"

"How about you?"

"They call me two or three times a week."

"Oh, that's—"

"Huh?"

"That's, that's nice. It must be—"

"Huh?"

When they get to the front of the line Glenn asks Vicky if she packed any aspirin. He settles for an antacid.

They put some makeup on Vicky and move her hair around a little bit and spray. They don't do anything to Glenn. "You look very nice," the Makeup girl tells him.

On their way back to Holding Glenn notices people eating snacks. He asks someone. The guy tells them where craft services is set up, right outside and around the corner. They find tables of breakfast items and snacks under tent frames in the shade. Glenn goes to the first table. He looks at the scrambled eggs and salsa. The man working behind the table looks at Glenn and tells him this section is for Crew only. He points to the other table where Vicky is toasting a half a bagel. "That one is for Extras." Glenn nods and anyone who can read faces would know that he has just learned an important fact about the distribution of amenities in the entertainment industry.

When they finish their bagels and get back to the Holding Area Sierra the 2nd AD is still at her desk with her list of names and is pointing at a young guy in the front row. "What's your name?"

"Costa."

"No, that isn't it." Laughter. One confused stare. "You're okay," she says going back to her list. "It's not you." Around 10:30 she announces that they need everybody on the set. "You've all used the restroom, right?" She leads them all across the street to the sound stage. Vicky is fidgety. Her phone is off and in her little wallet-like purse which is actually a purse-like wallet.

The sound stage if you look up is a migraine headache because there's no ceiling where a ceiling should be and it's gloomy up there behind the lights and they've put wires and pipes and fixtures and connecters and air ducts and scaffolding and acoustic panels in a strange jarring jumble that should be a scene out of a Hitchcock movie shot in black and white with screeching background music and sharp editing.

The sound stage if you don't look up is basically Department 123 of the Criminal Courts Building.

Glenn is not looking up. He is looking at the judge's bench and the counsel tables and the witness stand and the jury box and the wooden railing and the spectator gallery and the official seal and the flags. He is looking like a homesick American stumbling upon an American fast food franchise on a side street in downtown Wuhan. Glenn is looking like he just got to work after a hard day at home.

"Members of the Press, let's have you in these seats in the front. Court Staff, sit tight for a second we'll get you situated. Jurors, you can grab seats in the jury box. Spectators, just start filling in these rows for now. Quiet everyone." When she does a downward motion with her hands you get a nice view of some of Sierra's tattoos.

The inside of her right forearm says *Vida Mágica* in calligraphy, and a pentagram with an eye in the middle.

The Stovers take the last two places in the third pew of Spectators. They sit back with stiff shoulders against the hard maple. The courtroom around them has all the decorum and dignity of a construction site. While Vicky watches camera people and sound people and lighting people and set people and runners on walkie-talkies and nobody directing traffic, she looks like she regrets not wearing her hardhat. Glenn looks like a pair of earplugs would be a handy thing right now.

One of the PA's is standing in front of the Members of the Press and surveying. "You," she says, "why don't you change seats with him. Sit back in your seat. Yeah. You, uncross your legs. You, cross yours. No, go back to the way you were."

Vicky and Glenn are talking low and she is brushing lint off his pants. Sierra comes over and looks at them and then looks around and then looks at them. "Mmmmh," she says. "I think we're gonna switch you." She's talking to Vicky. She takes Vicky over to the jury box and makes Juror Number Eight give Vicky her juror badge. She brings the lady to the empty seat by Glenn. The lady seems a little deflated but she smiles at Glenn and he smiles back but not with his eyes. They are mostly focused on commiserating with Vicky's across a crowded courtroom.

When the actors come into the courtroom the faces of the extras flush a little bit and they watch the actors get their bearings and go through blocking with the 1st AD and the camera people and all the other crew keep doing the things they need to do but mostly they are asking each other how exactly what they're supposed to do should be done. Vicky whispers to Juror Number Nine, a young man with sandals, that isn't that the guy who played Sammy Davis, Jr. in that TV movie about his life. Juror Number Nine shrugs his shoulders. "George Something," Vicky says.

Eventually they're ready to do a couple run-throughs and then actual takes. They're shooting the victim's testimony. She's attractive. She's probably somebody, but Vicky doesn't have any biographic information to whisper. Ms. Tilden's testimony is not too controversial. She was mugged from behind, passed out and doesn't remember much of anything after that. Never got a look at the person. She sounds sad and cries a little. It's okay, she got to use her full emotional range when they shot the scene at the hospital.

During a slow moment between takes, the camera guy near Vicky starts a conversation with one of the cute young extras. The camera guy looks more like a movie star than the actors. He hasn't shaved for maybe two or three mornings. He should buy a bigger teeshirt. You have to be a bodybuilder to lift one of those cameras. There's an assistant camera guy whose job is to lift the camera onto the camera guy's shoulder pad. He just lifted it off. This is a break. The cute extra asks the camera guy if the shoulder pad takes the weight off his shoulder. He starts explaining. He touches her shoulder and then he touches the middle of her back to demonstrate. Her body stiffens and shrinks. She nods her head but her smile evaporates. Just a shadow lingers, frozen in place.

Vicky overhears this episode. She looks at Glenn but can't catch his eye. By the time they wrap a couple scenes at almost 2:30 she looks worn out.

Lunch is good. People aren't bashful in the least. A dapper guy with a healthy appetite sits down across from Glenn while he's waiting for Vicky to fill her tray. The guy starts talking about random but useful information related to being an extra. The guy has a slight stutter. He tells Glenn that it doesn't matter for this shoot but in general he should trim his eyebrows more. The guy does have lovely eyebrows.

Glenn likes the eggplant lasagna. He gets a kick out of the extras who brought little plastic containers to take home leftovers and think nobody notices. Vicky only eats foods without garlic. "How's my breath," she says before they take their places back in the courtroom.

"Fruity," says Glenn.

"That's my lip gloss."

"That's all I smell. You're acceptable."

"You could use a mint."

It takes a little while for everyone to wander in and find their places and get set. There's a new actress on the witness stand. The Director doesn't think they need any run-throughs for this scene. She keeps glancing at her phone. She asks one of the camera operators if they can see the District Attorney. She is sitting at some video monitors and talking normally so either she can throw her voice or she is talking into something. The Director is one of the people that Glenn is looking puzzled and watching. The others are the three people assembled around her who all look smart and important but no one knows exactly who they are and what they're doing there.

"I can see him," says the camera operator.

"Pan left two inches, Carl. Okay, stop. Who's that next to the bailiff?"

"That's Camera A."

"Okay, pan right two inches, Carl."

"Just moments away," says the 1st AD to the whole assembly. He seems to be very thoughtful of the feelings and anxieties of the extras. If he were a gynecologist he would be the kind that women have to wait a month to get an appointment with. They would like his eyes, too. "Okay, picture's up," he says. He adjusts his steel-rimmed glasses.

A little blonde PA is jumping up and down. "Let's do this, people."

"Roll sound," says the 1st AD.

"Sound rolling."

"Cameras?"

"A ready."

"B ready."

"C ready."

"Roll em."

Runners on and off the set repeat some of the directions into their walkie-talkies, like "camera rolling." There is shushing.

The scene board guy chops his sign for the camera. He says what scene it is. It has a letter and a number. People are blinking.

"All set? Background?" People are manually adjusting their breathing dial. Most of them have it set on Low. "ACTION."

"Ms. Watanabe." George Something approaches the witness. "What were you doing when the person you've identified as the Defendant ran into your pilates studio?" He could have pulled on his goatee, it might have been quite effective, but the choice he makes is sticking his thumbs in the buttonholes of his suit jacket and standing straight like somebody having their weight and height checked at the doctor's office. He does a head swivel toward the jury. The tall girl holding the boom is smiling. Juror Number Four squirms in her seat and her chair creaks. Sierra is crouching in a corner. She closes her eyes and mouths a word. It begins with the upper teeth biting the lower lip.

"Nothing," says the actress on the witness stand. "I was stretching out my hip flexors."

"That's odd," George Something says, "doesn't your own best-selling pilates video say that the hip flexors should be stretched first thing in the morning?"

"Uhhhh."

"Objection, Your Honor, that calls for hearsay. The video is not in evidence." The actor who used to play a crooked state senator on that show about the nineteen-year-old gay kid who becomes Governor of

Nebraska throws his pen down on his legal pad and glares at the first actor.

"It's not hearsay, Your Honor, we're simply exploring the veracity of this witness's identification of my client."

Glenn sits up straight like he's watching a tennis match of high lobs between opposing counsels.

"Sustained. Next question please."

"Sustained?" The whisper is a whisper but the whole cast and crew know they heard something, they just don't know what or where. The two extras on either side of Glenn look at him and then look at each other with fear in their eyes.

There's a shout from the 1st AD. "We're still rolling, let's reset, no talking." They start the scene again from the top. This time Glenn lets the judge rule without comment.

"Sustained. Next question please."

"Well," says the first actor, "were you expecting anyone at your studio at that particular time?"

"No. I didn't have another class til 3."

"So would it be fair to say that you were caught off guard when somebody dashed into your studio and out the back door?"

"Objection, argumentative," says the other guy.

"Sustained," says the actress in the black robe who probably got high marks for being able to portray malevolence when she was a theater major. "Rephrase, Mr. Singleton."

But George Something majored in understatement in acting school, and he does understated chagrin almost as well as Glenn is doing it as a first-time extra. "Well, Ma'am, what was your first reaction when this person suddenly raced through your studio?"

"I was afraid."

"Of what?"

"Of being raped."

"So what was your reaction, what did you do?"

"Nothing."

"Did you call the police?"

"No."

"Did you scream?"

"No."

"Did you leave the studio, go perhaps somewhere safer?"

"No."

"So you did nothing."

"Well, I went and looked out the back door. To see where he went."

"So you followed him?"

"Just to the alley."

"And was the man in the alley?"

"No. I didn't see him anywhere."

"He was nowhere in sight."

"No. I guess he was a very fast runner."

"You guess he was a very fast runner. Well I guess he was a very fast runner, too, Ms. Watanabe." This is where some of the extras have to chuckle derisively. It says so on page fifty-three of the script. "Your Honor, I have no further questions." He sits down and whispers to the actor in jail blues sitting next to him.

"Mr. Gunther, any redirect?"

"Ms. Watanabe, you wanted to get a good look at this person, didn't you, because your boyfriend is a police officer and you knew that they were looking for a serial rapist in your neighborhood?"

"Objection, leading and assumes facts not in evidence." Everyone freezes. Some people look like they just heard the wrathful voice of God. Vicky is on her feet gaping at her husband like the time he talked her into seeing Straw Dogs because Dustin Hoffman is her favorite actor. Glenn is standing at his spot in the gallery quivering and aghast. No one has ever seen Glenn aghast before. Everyone is looking back and forth between Glenn and the 1st AD.

"CUT," says the 1ˢᵗ AD like he's not too sure of anything at the moment including who or what he is. He stares at Glenn. "Am I missing a page from the—"

He is interrupted by a scream. Glenn is clutching his back and turning a garish shade of purple. No, Amethyst.

Ordinarily, talking to a screenwriter whose tendonitis has suddenly flared up would be a happy occasion for Glenn. Ordinarily, Glenn would have a clever answer to why he decided to become a movie extra. The fact that he's retired and trying to do some of the things he never had a chance to do before is probably not going to end up in any of the catchy dialogue that the writer is working on.

It's not like Glenn to look like someone with depression. But if the one person in the world who can read him better than anyone were here, who knows what her diagnosis would be.

The Nurse Practitioner is back at his cot. Glenn squints up at her and tells her for the second time in fifteen minutes that she looks familiar, from somewhere previous. While she's checking his ice pack she says she used to work at County Hospital. He shakes his head. He's been seeing people all day who look familiar and telling Vicky all about it and shaking his head.

"What do you usually take for your sciatica, Mr. Stover?"

"I just have to take it easy for a few days. I've tried things but, nah. This was not as bad as sometimes. Ahhhhhh!" Glenn's spine apparently didn't like the way he said that.

"Your wife said they're going to let her drive her car in and park behind the infirmary after they finish wrapping her scene."

He closes his eyes and settles into a breathing pattern gradually slowing and softening. Every once in a while the Nurse Practitioner checks on him and smiles.

About 5:30 Vicky gets to be the one to wake him up. She helps him to a sitting position, and then a standing one. She carries his discharge papers and valuables. The screenwriter is just checking out, too, and Glenn hands him a business card. He also hands one to the assistant editor who just came in with food poisoning from the ranch dressing at the cafeteria. He also hands one to the studio laundress who slipped and fell and is waiting for her daughter to pick her up and take her to Van Nuys for an x-ray of her ankle. In the movie business, or in life, you can never have too many friends. Your friends can never have too many technical consultants.

13

THIRTEEN

Before they detach a shopping cart, Vicky wants him to scratch her back. He looks around. They are theoretically in the way of traffic. Upscale supermarkets like Peddler Pete's don't always have more than one entrance. He starts scratching, through the material.

"Lower," she says. "No, higher."

A lady who looks like she's married to someone who does something creative in Hollywood is approaching the store and noticing them and smiling. The kind of smile that makes retired guys who are scratching their wife's backs feel pretty good.

While they're in the aisle with the frozen entrees at waist level and crackers at eye level, Glenn is telling Vicky about the current state of his itch receptors.

"And when I go to scratch it," he says, "I can't find the exact spot of the itch. It itches, but where?" Vicky doesn't tell Glenn that she's heard some of this story before. She listens and tries to find the brand of frozen eggplant parmesan that they usually buy. "So I just scratch the general area. It's very unsatisfying."

Someone in Vicky's support group has the same weird phenomenon, ever since her last chemo.

"Who, Polly?"

"No, Prashanthi."

"The funny thing is," he says, "it almost describes what life is like, at our age. Doesn't it, Vick? Sort of?"

She supposes that it does. She gives up on finding the eggplant and takes some assorted pot pies. Plus some chocolate covered almonds.

He dreamed that they invited Lydia and her husband over for dinner. It's the first time that Vicky's ever seemed interested in hearing him talk about his dreams. She props her pillows up against the headboard.

Glenn always listens to her dreams. She doesn't dream very much but when she does he seems to get a kick out of the way she tells them. Like the time she dreamed an entire documentary about global warming with interviews of flood victims in Iowa and starving Somali refugees. She thought it was a pretty good documentary. She told him at the time that she wondered if she could sell it to the National Geographic Channel.

"How were they dressed?"

"Nice," says Glenn. "She wore a pink dress and he wore his uniform. With a sword."

"A sword?"

"Yeah I don't know where that came from." He is squinting a little at the bright sunlight bouncing off their neighbors' white stucco and through their bedroom window.

She tells him that subconsciously he must feel the same way about them as she does.

He says he doesn't know, he doubts that they would have as much in common as she imagines, she might be idealizing them in her mind.

"Honey, Lydia works harder than anybody I've ever seen. She's a one-woman war against dirt, emblematic of her life. Just struggling to make it in this country."

There might be a language barrier, he says, her English is okay but can they have the kind of conversation that she really wants to have? "His English might not be good at all."

"She was a teacher in El Salvador, and he was a local police chief."

"I know."

"They fled for their lives because he had gone after corrupt cops in his department and he was shot at, threatened, etcetera."

"I didn't know about the part of being shot at. Sweetheart, how could you watch her slave away over your toilet bowl if they become our best friends? It's hard enough now to sit there while she mops and vacuums and wipes down everything in the house."

"So we'll be best friends and she won't work for us anymore."

"But she needs the job. You would take away part of her income so that she could be your friend?"

Vicky sinks her head back on her pillow and stares at the angled ceiling.

"If you start something with them, you don't know how it's gonna turn out."

"How did it turn out in your dream?"

"A lot of strange people started showing up and I couldn't find a vacant bathroom with a door that locked. I'll be right back."

When he comes back from the bathroom she has the covers kicked off. She is doing some of her morning stretching exercises. He watches her with his hands on his hips.

"God, all night long I have these crazy dreams," he says. "Half of them are about trying to find a space for me when there is no space. A workspace in a crowded room of desks. A room in a crowded dormitory, a corner to put my things in a room with too many people already. Why do I have these awful dreams?"

FOURTEEN

"Coming into your place. Leaving the world behind. Be here. And now. Breathe. Focus on your breath. If your mind wanders, acknowledge the thoughts and let them simply pass through and then return to the breath. If there's one thing you take away from this weekend it's to breathe and focus on your breath."

Everyone is supposed to be totally relaxed. Still. There are no sounds upstairs or in the kitchen. There is no street noise. There are no gardeners or trash collectors. Neighborhood dogs have nothing to bark at. There are no crows or scrub jays protesting the order of things. Just a few cheeping sparrows. And one hummingbird, maybe two if you were outside and your eyes could keep up. A mourning dove croons its early lullaby.

Glenn's feet are itching to wriggle just enough to keep the blood flowing. He wouldn't want to cause a spiritual incident. If his socks are generating tiny wooly crackles no one seems to hear them. They're at the end of his mat. He raises his head to look. His head is about fourteen

inches from the wall. His feet are about fourteen inches
from the head of the lady with the short silver ponytail
and her grandkids' pictures on her teeshirt. They were
probably cute kids once but the teeshirt has been washed
about seventy times. Glenn's socks are clean. He is clean.
After lunch he took a shower in the shower they're
sharing with four other people on their floor. The shower
had peach, pecan and nutmeg shampoo with a picture
of those three items on the label. The soap smelled even
better than the shampoo. Glenn had told Vicky that
he'd rather pay less for the weekend and have cheaper
toiletries. Also that if they took all the edible ingredients
in shampoo and deodorant and used them to feed
people they could end world hunger. Vicky's look was
one of suspicion.

Before class Vicky took video. She got the views
from the windows. She got all the memorabilia and
furnishings. She got some of the ladies smiling
and waving or blushing and hiding their faces. She
got a wide shot of the wall that's above Glenn's head.
She got the brick fireplace and the large inscription on
the wall that says Tarzana Mindfulness Institute and
has dates and names of founders.

"When you're ready, roll onto one side in a fetal
position and rest your head on your hands. And if you
want, you can set an intention for your practice today."

They do some leg lifting exercises and Glenn can
do them if you don't worry about the fact that he can't
straighten his legs more than halfway when they're
elevated into an inversion position. Vicky only peeks at
Glenn once in a great while. It would be embarrassing
to have to burst into hideous laughter in the middle of a
serious yoga class.

When they do some of the twists and arms in a T,
their arms touch and Glenn likes to let the touch linger.
Once Glenn's arm touches his other neighbor's arm and
they both flinch. "Sorry." There are seventeen people

doing yoga in this room. They call it The Sunroom. Johnny Weissmuller probably did handstands here.

"And in yoga, only do what feels right to you. This is your practice. If something doesn't feel right or is painful, then listen to your body."

Glenn can't bend at the waist. That's obvious when they do the standing and bending exercises. Vicky is very limber. So when Vicky is bending and Glenn is only tilting he can stare a little at the only young woman in the group. Her body and yoga outfit seem to lead him spiritually in the direction of inner peace.

After they wind down with some sitting exercises Corinne the yoga teacher says how gratifying it is that two gentlemen are here for this retreat. "Usually," she says, "we are thrilled to have even one guy join us. So we are really blessed to have two wonderful spouses in our midst this weekend. And such sweet guys. I wish all husbands were more like you two."

Paul is the other guy in the group. He looks like he could have been Johnny Weissmuller's stunt double once upon a time. Apart from the fact that Johnny was one of the few stars who probably never needed a stunt double. When Corinne aims her adoring spotlight at the two husbands Paul does a good job of smiling and having perfect posture and being polished like a hotel mirror. Glenn does a better job at being funny and putting his empty palms up. Most of the ladies' heads are turned toward the shiny mirror. The empty palms get maybe two or three, probably the ones with the worst cataracts.

Vicky grabs her pillow for *Shavasana* and leans over to tell Glenn in his ear that he should see how big his head just got. Glenn shrugs and does his mouth like Maurice Chevalier. Chevalier was the best of all the movie gigolos at assuming innocence. *Shavasana* is Glenn's favorite part of yoga.

Corinne thinks that since they're spending the weekend in
Johnny Weissmuller's first house in Hollywood it would
be fun and would help them all get to know each other
to make the theme of tonight's rap session something
splashy and nostalgic: Mindfulness and the Movies.
"Why don't we begin by going around the room and you
can each introduce yourself and tell us a little bit about
yourself. And then we'll jump into tonight's exercise. And
don't forget that we'll cap the night off with after-dinner
liqueurs and ice cream in the library, courtesy of
the Institute."

"We're all going to sleep very well tonight."

"That's right, Sophia, so no one will have any excuse
for being tired tomorrow." To teach yoga you don't have
to have a face that can't help being cute and funny but it
makes things less clumsy. "Anyway, I hope you all read
the handout that we left in each room. The idea is to
describe a movie scene that works for you as a guided
imagery. Most of you are familiar with guided imagery."
It's also nice that Corinne is one of those people who can
talk to a group and move her eyes around just the right
amount so that no one has to worry about prolonged eye
contact with the speaker but no one has to worry about
being left totally out of the connection either. Corinne
and her eyes tell the group that they're each going to
describe some memorable movie scene that captured their
heart, perhaps, the first time they saw it. And now, she
says, it might be a perfect image to focus on when they
want to reach a state of mindfulness and deep relaxation.
She calls on a lady named Roxie to start the introductions
off and says it's because Roxie has been on a few of her
other retreats in previous years. Then they'll go clockwise
around the room. "Okay?" Vicky and Glenn are

practically twelve hours from Roxie so Glenn only looks mildly terrified when he catches Vicky's eye.

She's Roxie and she's taken Corinne's class at the YMCA in Sherman Oaks for about four and a half years. "I'm hopelessly addicted to yoga and the retreats are the best things you can ever do. I'm ecstatic to be here." Roxie looks like Ruth Gordon in Harold and Maude only more limber.

"Hi, I'm Robyn. This is my first retreat though I've known Corinne for many years through our kids. Our kids more or less grew up together." Corinne finally twisted her arm to where she couldn't say no anymore and now she's a yoga beginner and here she is at an actual retreat. "Yay."

"Sophia?"

"I'm Sophia Rogers and I'm not sure if I'm the oldest person here but I'm definitely the crankiest. Just ask Corinne."

"It's true."

"And I'm really here just for the crème de cocoa and toffee ice cream."

"Mmmh, that sounds so good. I'm Petra and this is my husband Paul, and yoga was really Paul's idea. Once we both retired he thought it would be something healthy that we could both do together. I have back issues and he has problems with his knees and Corinne has done wonders for both of us. Thank you, Corinne."

Paul clears his throat and agrees with his wife and says he doesn't have much to add except that he feels very lucky to be there and everybody's so friendly which is unusual in Los Angeles. "This is like a little sanctuary from the crazy world out there. I wish it could last." Glenn's face is where the guy's eyes come to rest. If he were paying attention Glenn would have reason to wonder but Glenn is looking down like he's got a closing statement to give to a jury in five minutes about why

the felony murder rule applies to negligent discharge
of a firearm.

"I like that thought, Paul." says Corinne. "If we work
at it, we will hopefully have the tools to create our own
inner sanctuary, no matter where we are or how crazy it
gets. Rita?"

Three of the people pick scenes from The Sound of
Music, one picks Doctor Zhivago driving a troika over
the snow in Siberia with the theme music playing. One
lady had a spiritual experience when she saw On Golden
Pond. And one lady's special mindfulness fantasy is that
she's playing with Bambi and Thumper with "Little April
Showers" drip-dropping all around. She causes two other
people to snap their fingers because they didn't pick that
one and now it's too late. It's already taken.

The only person who picks a foreign film is Paul. It's
the very last shot from The Seventh Seal with the little
family and the horse and the sun shining on the sea. He
never forgot it, it changed his life.

Vicky picks one of the lush garden scenes from
Atonement. She's walking in the garden with a cup of tea
and a handsome soldier.

Glenn describes a scene he wishes he could identify.
It was in an old Saturday Afternoon at the Movies black
and white picture he's never heard of or seen since. He
was the only one in the TV room in the basement and
their basement was a little spooky and he was probably
eight. The scene was about five minutes and strange
shadowy half-naked figures were just standing in this
murky kind of jungle while the lead actor who he can't
identify wandered through the place in a bewildered state.
Not a word was spoken. He doesn't know why or what
was happening or anything else about the picture. But
it's stuck in his mind. Vicky looks surprised while Glenn

is talking, like moms look when they catch their kids
practicing the piano without being told.

Vicky doesn't want coffee with her ice cream. She's
watching Sophia, that lady with the comedic timing
who probably wins comedy night at the Senior Center,
arranging the fancy liqueurs, unscrewing the caps, sniffing
and rolling her eyes.

Glenn goes to the kitchen with the Institute cup
he picked out to be his cup for the weekend. It says
"Everything you need is already within you."

"I hope it's not decaf, huh Glenn?" Glenn turns
around. Paul's cup only says COFFEE. "Can't let our
wives catch us nodding off, can we?" he says.

Glenn says he might have to carry his wife upstairs
later on if they don't lock up those creamy liqueurs
pretty soon. He asks Paul what he did before he retired.
Something to do with men's clothing or something?
Glenn looks almost sincere when he says it, almost like he
really would like to know.

Paul's head is shaking, he's a portrait of tragic woe.
"Have I changed that much?" Glenn's eyebrows don't
know whether they heard the other guy correctly. "You
don't remember me at all, do you?"

Glenn has to put his coffee on the counter. He says
something about being sorry and he, uh. He doesn't, uh.

"August, 1982?"

Glenn's head tilts. His eyes drift upwards toward the
regions where lost riddles can be spun and unspun. He
repeats the date almost silently.

"Judge Niemeyer?"

Glenn's forehead is going to start to hurt eventually.
No one can concentrate that hard for more than
ten seconds.

"I had a public defender named Hilts?"

"You're saying I prosecuted you?"

"How can you not remember?" The redder the guy's face gets the more it seems to sting. "You sent me to jail for three hundred sixty-five days. You told my attorney you would ask the judge for four years in prison if I didn't plead guilty."

"Well, I—I'm sorry, I just don't remember. I don't disbelieve what you're saying, I just can't remember every case I had thirty-five years ago. I barely remember what I had for breakfast."

"So," says Paul, "I should have kept my big mouth shut."

Why did he bring it up, Glenn wants to know. So the guy says he assumed Glenn would have remembered him and he didn't want him to say anything in front of his wife. She doesn't know. That was before they met. "She doesn't know I ever used drugs, let alone got busted for sales," he says.

"Man," says Glenn. "That's rough. You got kids, too?"

"A married son."

"Sales, huh?"

"I wasn't a pusher, Glenn. I just sold enough to support my—well you know the score, I don't have to tell you. Don't get me wrong, I have no grudge against what you did. You did your job and, and maybe it was the best thing. It scared me clean, I never went back to that stuff. I think the system worked, at least for me."

"I wish I had that much faith in it," Glenn says. He says he won't give the guy away. He's been married so many years and he's an honest man and family man, seems to have a nice marriage, they do yoga together for god's sake, no reason to dig up ancient history.

Paul is practically crying, slaps Glenn on the back and tells him with a kind of hysterical laugh that he'll buy him a cup of coffee. Glenn picks up his cup. He takes a sip and his expression says that cold coffee's pretty good for a change.

"It looks like our husbands have hit it off," says Petra in the library. Her hot fudge sundae is now just vanilla cream soup with swirls of chocolate lava.

"Crikey it does, fair dinkum," says Vicky. She sips from her glass of Australian ouzo. She closes her eyes. If anyone has ever looked like they're doing guided imagery in the garden from Atonement, it's Vicky. It looks like she found a friend in that garden.

After "lights out" everyone is supposed to be mindful about keeping the noise down to a level that doesn't travel beyond the walls of their individual rooms. Given the name of the place and the reason why they're there, this is a rule that seems easy for everyone to swallow and there is no dissent from any quarter of the house where Tarzan once laid his head, probably after yodeling a little. The toilet is down the hall so flushing is the implied exception. "Lights out" is at 10 pm.

"It's 10:45."

"So?"

"You asked me what time it was."

"When?"

"At 10:45. How much brandy did you drink?"

"None. It was ouzo. Hardly has any alcohol."

"Oh. That's why you're wearing your sweatpants inside out?"

"I am not. Oh, I am. No, I'm just really tired."

"All that yoga."

"Wasn't it great? Aren't they great?"

"Yeah, great group."

"No, Petra and Paul, aren't they great?"

"Yeah nice uh, nice couple."

"She is so sincere, we laughed so much. And you two guys are great, you had a nice conversation together. You seem to have a lot in common, personality and everything."

"Mmmmh."

"Don't you feel like you kind of bonded?"

Vicky is lying down, she can't see Glenn's face while he sits at the desk by the window and sorts his bedtime pills like they're the kind you take if you're captured by the enemy. Only the desk lamp is lighted and Vicky is in shadows. "I wouldn't exactly—"

"I think we should plan something with them. They love going out, doing things."

"He's a lot more talkative than I am."

"He doesn't talk too much, why do you say that, you're wrong you talk more." Vicky's bed is a single bed built into one wall. Glenn's is built into the other wall. The other wall rises darkly across eight feet of floor which is varnished pinewood and, like many wood floors, sleeps with a throw rug. Glenn hasn't pulled down the covers that he will have to pull down if he ever decides to sleep. The covers are smooth, a quilty bedspread with a regulated pattern of faded red flowers and green leaves. Those little printed bouquets and a white creamy background have obviously talked business and settled upon pink as the net effect of their creative partnership. A little girl with dolls and a book about adventures in babysitting should be in that bed. Maybe she was, once, and scattered some of those faded red flowers onto the throw rug where they stuck. Vicky rips off her covers and looks stressed and flushed. In a room with a couch like a psychiatrist's, a ball chair, pastoral paintings, framed pithy affirmations like "I attract positive energy", hanging chimes and a mallet, music boxes, lava lamps, a fish aquarium softly bubbling, lavender, rubber squeeze balls, something like playdough, and sleep masks, you are not supposed to be stressed and flushed.

"I don't mean talkative like more words," Glenn says, "I mean he's more into talking as a—" It's a good swallow, one of his pills should have hopped on. "—thing."

"You mean he's more into having actual contact with other humans and making friends with a few of them."

Glenn says no and calls Vicky Sweetheart and says that's not what he's trying to say. "I don't think he listens to classical music at all."

"You talked about music?"

"We didn't have to. He lifts barbells, for crying out loud. He drives a Land Rover."

"How do you know he doesn't listen to Beethoven while he—oh for god's sake."

"Vick, he looks like Robert Redford on steroids. How do you think that makes me—"

"So you only want friends who are ugly?"

Glenn puts his head down into the palm of his left hand. An owl hoots somewhere nearby. Another answers from farther away. When the crickets die down you can hear the faint purr of the freeway. "Don't you think Palos Verdes is too far away to start up a relationship?"

Vicky says she thought he would be glad they didn't live too close.

"What if there were another—nevermind." He sits for a while staring at the row of books on the desk between big scented candles for bookends. The books are dust-free and look like they've never been opened. The *Mindful Mystique* by Ted Rascioli has something with water and rocks on the cover but the candle is in the way. Glenn gazes into the night with the moral righteousness of an anonymous hero, saving the world, sacrificing his own life and legacy. Finally he turns out the lamp and gets into his bed. Then out again. His stockings test the pinewood floor which is a solid sleeper except for one fussy plank in the middle.

It's dark and she may be asleep. But she's not. Glenn leans in for a goodnight kiss and has to feel around for Vicky's mouth because it's as far from a state of pucker as she can zip it.

Vegan Chef Valadez is the youngest person in the room. He is also the only one with a moustache. He wishes everyone good morning and trails one hand along the buffet and identifies all the dishes. "Chickpea and teff pancakes with sundried tomatoes and peppers topped with avocado and spicy cashew cream. Blueberry oatmeal waffles and orange banana compote. Warm and nutty cinnamon quinoa granola. Braised wild asparagus and mushrooms. Homemade jelly muffins and scones. And detox green monster smoothie. Please, enjoy." The last item gives a red blush to some people in the group and its own color to some of the others. Glenn raises his eyebrows at Vicky, who is staring at Chef Valadez's white chef uniform that has no sauce or juice or compotes on it. The whole group is lined up around the giant dining room table to hear announcements and some words of yoga wisdom. Mrs. Wolfe, the Tarzana Mindfulness Institute hostess for the weekend, announces that the Jacuzzi has stopped working but they're hoping to have it fixed before the retreat ends that evening and everyone checks out. She looks out the window and says the low clouds should burn off by noon. Then she has a big mindful grin when she calls on the two husbands to be the servers and clearers for this meal. Everybody laughs. Everybody usually laughs in yoga groups when guys get singled out. Most of the able-bodied women had already volunteered at one of the other meals. Vicky and Petra did Saturday dinner. The meals are all buffet so the only things to serve are water pitchers and hot sauce. Clearing means bussing the tables and rinsing the dishes with a spray nozzle in an industrial size sink in the kitchen and stacking them for the staff to wash later. Ten minutes tops.

Corinne reminds everyone about the morning yoga session which will be restorative yoga which everyone seems relieved to hear and about the late afternoon happy hour and talk by the guy who brought mindfulness to the west coast. She folds her hands over her heart and closes her eyes. "The world exists as you perceive it." Everyone stands up straight with their feet together and folds their hands and closes their eyes. "It is not what you see but how you see it. It is not what you hear but how you hear it. It is not what you feel but how you feel it. *Namaste*."

"*Namaste*."

The two couples sit together for the meal and the wives want to know about how the other couple met and their whole life story. Vicky goes first and it's a cute story and Glenn gets to act kind of smug and sanctimonious when Vicky gets to the part about the double date and how she immediately forgot about her date and started to monopolize this skinny, sardonic young lawyer named Glenn Stover when the couples met at the Mexican restaurant on Santa Monica that the two guys had picked out and which isn't there anymore and which seems to be a bad location for restaurants because each one that opens up lasts a few years and that's all. Glenn does most of the talking about their kids and Vicky is watching him closely to make sure he makes them sound successful in the way that all couples try to make their kids sound outstanding and never disappointing when it comes to academic achievements and professional careers and romantic attachments and any other distinctions they might have.

"We met at the gym," says Petra. "I never really liked guys with big muscles but Paul's were just like Marlon Brando, very natural like he was born with them." Vicky bites her lower lip with glee and watches her friends make flaring eyes at each other. Glenn stands up and bumps the table and rattles dishes and causes water glasses to slosh over. He goes to get another waffle. And extra napkins.

"Six months later we were married."

"Oh my." Vicky wants to know about their wedding and their families and what kind of work they did when they were young. Petra was a hairdresser and was trying to get signed on to movies or TV shows. Then she got pregnant.

"I was a lifeguard, down in Orange County," says Paul. "Seems like a million years ago. That's what I did back in Auckland before I immigrated. When I met Petra I was already starting to learn the cable business."

"I remember Glenn once prosecuted a professional lifeguard from Australia," says Vicky. She's dragging the tip of an asparagus spear around in the juicy regions of her plate. "A long long time ago. Or was it New Zealand?"

Glenn flinches and ceases the mopping operation around his glass. Slowly he shakes his head with the shock of ice water on the face. "I have no recollection of that."

"See, I remember these things."

Glenn employs a furtive glance to check on Paul. Glenn was never good at furtive glances. The other guy is maintaining eye contact with his deviled egg and there is something sticky and hard to swallow in his granola.

"You're thinking of a movie we saw once," Glenn says, "she remembers details from movies like they happened yesterday. Heh. She remembers every date we had when we were dating. Where we sat, what we were wearing. Even—"

"Well those are the things that really matter, aren't they, Glenn?" Petra flashes Vicky a loyal smile.

"I think so," says Vicky. She asks Paul how he got interested in cable television. And did he know it was going to take off like it did.

"You can take the Fifth, Paul," Glenn says. Paul forces a laugh. He gives Glenn an accusatory look like what's-his-name in that picture about the guy who has to take the murder rap for the other guy because the other guy once saved his life at Anzio.

Half of the group have already finished their breakfast and stood up and left the dining room. Glenn decides it's time to start clearing everybody's dishes and wiping the tables and Vicky does that thing with the lips of her mouth that women do when out of nowhere their torpid husbands take responsibility and show the kind of initiative that husbands do in bestsellers and on television. Paul carries a huge armload of dirty dishes to the kitchen and Glenn takes frequent trips with a plate and some silverware, maybe a glass. They work silently, looking down. The girls are giggling about something and trying each other's dessert. They glance at their husbands and smile to themselves. Then they smile at each other.

The sun just sank into the Santa Monica Mountains and fog is boiling over into the Valley like the foam from a vast pot of poached eggs. Paul finds Glenn by the cars, sweeping dust and redwood needles off his car with a combination ice scraper and snow brush. Paul looks around and they have the parking area to themselves. "Thanks for, you know. Being cool about the past." He is carrying four suitcases, two under each arm. His teeshirt says Newport, but it doesn't say which one. Glenn's teeshirt says the name of his high school.

Glenn watches the guy pack the trunk of his Cadillac. "No problem."

"You know, under different circumstances I bet we could have been pretty good friends." It's a big trunk, he doesn't need to have a system.

Glenn stands there letting a couple beats go by. "I don't think so, Paul." Paul turns and squints. "You like the Giants, I like the Dodgers. It never would have worked out." He shakes the guy's hand. Nothing wrong with the handshake, the guy goes easy on him.

"*Namaste.*"

"What does that mean, anyway?" says Glenn.

Paul unfolds his hands from his heart and goes to meet the girls, who are coming down from the house with their yoga mats and purses. There is plenty of time for Glenn to brush off the hood and windshield of the Cadillac while everybody hugs the wives and Paul slaps Glenn on the back and Vicky reminds Petra to send her the pictures she took and everybody reminds each other to drive safely and everybody nods as if they're the safest driver in California and safety is their number one priority.

One last little wave between the two girls and four car doors slam. Glenn finds his sunglasses.

"We saw you shaking hands from the porch."

"I went easy on him, I didn't want to hurt the guy."

"Very thoughtful of you."

"That's just the kind of guy I am." He backs out of his parking slot.

"Johnny Weissmuller had a big driveway."

"Uh-huh," Glenn says.

"Elephants," Vicky says.

FIFTEEN

It's not a big car, as cars go, which they do. When they started out, he put his seat back to get leg room in front. He forgot to say something. For a second one of her knees was wedged. It's okay now. She can reach forward and pick the fine blond strands from the shoulders of his suit, where they shed sunlight. The malls and office buildings along the 405 are tall but the sun is even taller.

"It was very irresponsible to get a dog when neither of you is home for most of the day and you have a tiny apartment and—"

"Mom, she would have been euthanized, and we didn't know our schedules would get so crazy."

The gift is professionally wrapped. It's a dozen personalized Champagne flutes. It's on the seat between Michelle and her mom. They're both photo ready, Michelle helped Vicky with her makeup after she did her own. They don't look like themselves. They can't smile without smudging something.

"And her hair is everywhere." She flicks then shakes all her fingers with phobic vigor. "Couldn't you have gotten a dog that doesn't—"

"That person has a Lamborati," says Glenn. "See? Look at her license plate. FLEET FILLY. Isn't that cute? And so intelligent to put that on your license plate with all the sexual predators around. I'm so glad she has that brand new sleek shiny Lamborati. She really needed that pretty bad."

"Dad."

"Her life would have been pretty sad if she didn't have that new hundred thousand dollar car to go shopping in."

"Dad."

He leans under the windshield for a closer look. "It's a Model S. I think my great-grandfather had a Model T. A little better looking than this lady's car but I'm sure it gets you where you wanta go." His wife and daughter look at each other in the manner of two brave nausea sufferers.

"Anyway, Honey, in your current circumstance the right thing to do is to find a better home for her."

"Peter loves her, Mom, he'd never think of giving her away."

"I'll take her. Until you get settled or something."

"We can't hear you back here, Sweetheart, you're talking away from us."

"I said I'll take her, Mom." Ryan has the confidence of a man with power steering in his hands, his eyes on the road and traffic opening up ahead.

"Like you took care of Edgar?"

"Mom, Edgar was a gecko, and I was eleven."

Glenn says this is just temporary and not a big deal. "An extended doggie visit. We're just dog sitting," he says.

"Mom?" says Michelle.

"I'm not cleaning up her messes."

"She'll be fine, she's almost housebroken. She's part of the family, after all." Glenn looks back at Michelle.

"Mmmmh," says Vicky.

Ryan glances at his dad. "I see a resemblance".

"Anyway, little kids love dogs. What? What's that look?"

"What look?" Vicky knows what look.

"I'm just saying kids love dogs, what's so bad about saying that kids love—"

"You're not very subtle, Grandpa."

"Dad."

"I'm just kidding, Sweetheart, you and Peter will decide when you're ready and if you're ready. It's your life, you hafta—"

"Glenn."

Michelle announces the fact that Peter had a vasectomy.

"No way." Ryan is the only one finding a glimmer of humor in the subject.

"He did what?"

"That was before we ever met. He just felt strongly that he had no right to bring children into such a violent world. It was a moral choice."

"A pretty drastic one, I'd say."

"Dad. It's not the end of the world. We're not even married yet. Aren't you jumping the gun?"

"Glenn, they could certainly adopt."

"I guess you knew all about this."

"They've given you Claudia. At least temporarily. You said she's like family."

"Somehow when I think of family I picture a granddaughter who I could take for walks by her hand, not a leash."

Ryan wants to know if he should take La Tijera or Century.

Glenn says Century. He thinks it's one of the first hotels.

"I think I'll take La Tijera."

"We'll be a little early," Vicky says. "I told you we could have left at four."

"Honk at that idiot, Ry." He gives Ryan half a second and then reaches over himself and bears down hard on the horn. "Didn't even signal, waited to the last second to get over two lanes."

"It's okay, Dad. We're fine."

"Came that close to our left headlight. Has the nerve to put a Save The Narwhal bumper sticker on his tail end. Look, he's stopped at the red light just like us. So what did he gain from that little stunt?"

"Close your eyes Glenn and do your guided imagery."

He closes his eyes and rests his head back. Michelle looks at her mom and Vicky says it's okay in pantomime. Glenn's eyes soon pop open. "Are you following him on purpose?"

"No Dad, I don't know, he's going where we're going."

Glenn says "Lucky us." He says "That's it" and points to the Airport Tower Hotel. "Not valet." He puts his hand up like a card player standing pat.

"Self-park?" Vicky frowns. That she can do with makeup.

They climb four levels to the roof. There's the black SUV that cut them off, just parking, about six spots away. Glenn gets out, walks quickly over to that car.

"Dad!"

"Glenn!"

"Hi, how're you doing?" Glenn takes off his sunglasses. He has a small smile but the man in the tuxedo stands at his open driver's door and stiffens. "I'm Glenn." He puts his hand forward. The man looks suspicious and glances at his wife. He has no choice but to shake. "What's your name?"

"I'm Isaac."

"You have a nice day, now, Isaac. Drive safe." Glenn walks back to his car, Gary Cooper in *High Noon* with all eyes staring wide.

It's a sweeping shot. The salads, the seafood, nuts and berries and sweets, a dozen different gourmet cookies and pastries. Tropical fruits shaped into a tropical paradise. Cantaloupes and watermelons cut like stars and wheels and flowers, not for eating just atmosphere. Persian vegetable patties, green ones and brown ones. Hummus and flatbread. Tea samovars. Put to the right music, the kind that makes you think of belly dancers and indigestion, the hors d'oeuvre buffet will make for a colorful opening. People love that, seeing those fancy spreads. The lady behind the big camera is wearing a purple evening dress with long earings and a necklace with a Star of David. She takes aim at some of the early guests, mostly American, their plates loaded and their mouths chewing in ways that might be regretted when the video comes out. Maybe she'll edit out the shots of Glenn and Ryan piling full course meals on their little plates.

"The sushi's not bad," Glenn says to Vicky.

"I think I'll wait."

Vicky uses her phone to record the same sights as the big camera. She and Michelle stay out of official camera range and she has Michelle say something nice to her phone for Uncle Phil and Aunt Shadi. Then the video lady and her lighting guy move on down the hallway. They look like Channel 6 News at the mayor's press conference about money that wasn't laundered, as far as he knew. Down the hallway, past the table where you turn in your gifts, there's a hotel meeting room set up for the ceremony. Regular people aren't allowed in yet. There's whispering about pictures being taken and everything being behind schedule. The Airport Tower Hotel has two other meeting rooms just like this one that has a sign that says Yaghoubian-Davidson Wedding. Vicky and Michelle pick up plates and look like they're pretty sure the food they're about to eat came from the same general place as the mayor's money.

One of the other two meeting rooms has a Trombo fundraiser going on, and the other has a meeting of the Santa Monica and West L.A. Genealogy Society. Those two events don't have lavish hors d'oeuvre buffets set up in the hallways, and their doors are closed. When the doors of the Yaghoubian-Davidson Wedding room open many people grab the arms of family members and merge into the only traffic lane that isn't shut down by CalTrans. But people are signaling and frequently waiving their right of way, so no one gets hurt.

The camera shoots the wedding procession from the front right corner. The Stovers have good seats, in the back. It's no problem seeing the attendants go down the aisle, there's a raised platform all the way. The aisle is roped off. The attendants don't walk down the runway. They have to dance. There's Persian music with rhythm. It's compelling. The people clap to the music. They whoop and whistle. About thirty or forty percent of the people have their phones out and are getting the whole thing. It's a different song for each pair. They make very attractive couples. There's an extra groomsman, though. He dances with flair, the people laugh and smile at each other. His weight doesn't seem to hinder his dancing. It seems to add mass to velocity. The groom is already up front under the canopy. He looks very handsome but nobody knows how he got there, or when. Shadi and Phil are seated up front. Vicky keeps straining her neck to see how they're holding up.

The wedding video will show everyone thought the ceremony was a real hoot. Even the bride and groom. Vicky is clapping along with everyone. Glenn mostly looks at the other guests around him and how they're enjoying everything. He looks at Vicky and his kids. "Why," he wants to know, "do they—" He freezes when Vicky quivers her head at him like they're being watched.

She darts her eyes around. Her hair is styled and swept over like Natalie Wood in *Splendor in the Grass*. When the bride finally comes down the aisle with her parents the music isn't for dancing. It's for walking and they walk with pride. Past about four hundred white wooden folding chairs, past white flowers and white pedestals. This is a very bright, glaring kind of space. Standing now, the guests all applaud and cheer. The bride smiles and beams. The video lady moves to a better angle for the ceremony. The Rabbi waits for her to signal him. He draws the young couple in close under the canopy.

The Rabbi seems nice and says some fine things about love and marriage and God but he doesn't get into anything specific about the bride or groom that would show that he has any first-hand acquaintance with them or what kind of kids they are or what they've done in their lives. But after a little while he gives them a chance to recite their own vows. They seem sincere.

"Jason," says Sheila, "ever since I first got to know you when we were counselors at Camp Nageela, I knew that there was something special and amazing about you and that fate may have brought us together for a reason. I felt that for the first time in my life I was complete. You make me laugh. Even now." And everyone does after Jason makes a face. "You make me cry with joy and tenderness." She is looking forward to their life together. She promises Jason all the things that probably swirl inside young couples' heads when they think about lives together. "I want to laugh and cry and love and live with you, Jason Davidson, and make you the happiest man in the world."

"Sheila, how can I find the words to tell you how happy you have made me?" Jason finds quite a few good words. Some of them are funny but most of them are humble and thankful and the guests get a little moister and so do their hankies or their top knuckles. "Sheila, you are my Cleopatra and I am your slave. You are the leading lady in a storybook romance and I am the luckiest leading man ever. But seriously, as long as I can be with you, by your side, I'm happy. Content. And grateful. I love you on this, our wedding day, and every other day. Those words are from this heart, and this heart is yours."

Just to make sure, the Rabbi also has his own set of vows as a backup. Will Jason take Sheila to be his wife, does he commit himself to her happiness and self-fulfillment as a person, does he promise to love, honor, and trust her in sickness and in health, in adversity and prosperity, and be true and loyal to her so long as they both shall live? He does.

Will Sheila take Jason to be her husband, and does she make all the other commitments and pledges? She does.

A couple of uncles come up and read Hebrew prayers and there's a lot of kissing of heads, mostly the groom's. The Rabbi has the groom and bride each repeat the Hebrew blessing while they do the rings. Then the cantor sings something. Then he puts a prayer shawl over their heads and the Rabbi has them drink from the wine cup. Then there's some fussing around for a few minutes and a moment of hesitation and then Jason breaks the glass in a white bag. He may have knee problems down the road.

Then everyone sings the mazeltov and simantov song and claps and dances a little before they let the young smiling couple anywhere near the door. Some men and boys in black fedoras come out of nowhere and seem even happier than the newlyweds.

Table number 6 is not any of the tables that Vicky and Glenn can find but Ryan shows up and has the numbering system figured out. Glenn acts disappointed that their table is not farther back in a corner somewhere but Vicky acts satisfied.

"I'm Brian," says the man at their table reaching across to shake. "This is my wife, Beverly." According to the tilt of the guy's left ear, it's a matter of fiduciary trust to remember the names that Glenn and Vicky give him. He says something about how they stuck all the Americans at one table.

"How do you know we're not Iranian?"

"That's a good one, Glenn." The ice cubes in the guy's bourbon have a chance to recede like little glaciers while he finishes laughing. His wife asks what their connection is.

Vicky explains that Phil is her brother. "The groom's father."

"Sure, we know who Phil is," says Brian. "But why aren't there more Americans here?"

Vicky says they have a very small family.

"Well, it's a very nice family."

"You must be connected with Phil's lodge or Jason's work or something."

"No, no. Sheila the bride is my executive assistant."

Glenn says "Oh". He thought his nephew was marrying an accountant.

"Well she will be, one of these days," says Brian. "I'm a CFO."

"Oh, okay. What kind of company are you with?"

"I'm with Pyramid Pictures. And yourself?"

Glenn's face looks like the man said Pyramid Cheese. Vicky looks at Glenn like something should have ticked but didn't. The music has started up and other couples join their table. Glenn fiddles with his box of earplugs, passes the salt to the person passing the walnuts in water, and shells pistachios on a plate. Vicky drinks her wine, makes small talk, and sends frequent glances across goblets, saucers, centerpieces and swathed tables to the three wedding guests out of five hundred who happen to be members of her immediate family.

115

They're having a little trouble with the buffet. Glenn's problem is that it's a lot of food and he keeps asking Vicky if this is dinner or not and she keeps shrugging her shoulders. Vicky's problem is that there are a million people thronged around and some of them fill their plates and then stand there and eat right in front of the buffet tables without moving. She tries to get up to the fresh cut fruit and olives and lavash and hummus but all she can get are glimpses. Same story with the fancy lush salads. She ends up with sweets, nuts, dried fruit and deep reddish tea that smells like licorice.

Glenn goes to get a drink at the bar and they meet back at the table and Glenn has big enough heaps of some kind of potato salad and some kind of egg salad and something like latkas only yellower to share with Vicky. Early Beatles is what the orchestra is playing. There is contentment in Glenn for the first time this evening.

The orchestra stops in the middle of a Dionne Warwick song. Glenn doesn't like it when Dionne Warwick songs are stopped in the middle. Glenn doesn't like radio stations that don't let songs finish to the last dying bar or talk over them. He started boycotting those stations when he was about nineteen. "Ladies and gentlemennnnnnnn," says a guy in a violet tuxedo. He's too young to remember the *Fight of the Week* on Saturday nights in black and white from Madison Square Garden. "May I have your attentionnnnnnnn. Thank you. Thank you. It is my honorrrr, to welcome all you beautiful people to the elegant, charming, dazzling Imperial Room of the incomparable Airport Tower Hotellllllllll." Glenn is checking to see if his earplugs have slipped. His watch says eight-fifteen. "We are here to celebrate the weddinggggg of the cennnnturyyyyy, the fantastic, unforgettable wedding of Jason and Sheila Davidsonnnnnnnn." Thundering applause. Whistles, cheers, screaming. Nobody knows who this guy is or how much he's getting paid or whether he gets to eat before everybody else or after everybody else but he has the microphone and he has a little bit of an accent and everybody seems to accept the fact that he is running the show. "First up I want you to show your appreciation for the Bride's parents and younger brother. Farzad, Leila and Jonathonnnnnnn". Under a huge spotlight and dance music these notables make an entrance. "Next, give it up for the parents of the Groom, Philip and Shadiiiiiiii." Jason's parents' faces have smiles almost like Sheila's parents but also a deep flush.

"And now, without further adieu, for the very first time as husband and wife, I want you all to bring the house down for the Bride and Groom themselves, Mr. and Mrs. Jasonnnnnnnnnn Davidsonnnnnnnnnnnnnnnn." Enter the royals. Amid thunderclaps, the newlyweds are brilliantly perfect. They are ready for the Hollywood Bowl and maybe they could have staged their first dance there at half the cost of the wedding but it seems like this is the venue at which they would rather star. Glenn might have picked something by Ella Fitzgerald but the Bride and Groom are dancing to a Disney song about a magic carpet ride. Glenn tells Vicky's earring that he didn't know Jason could dance. Vicky is videoing the whole thing. In the middle she pans left for a second to get the side of Glenn's face.

Pretty soon the dance floor is full and the tempo speeds up. The sound level ramps up with each new number. With serious eyes looking for ominous signs, Glenn watches. The orchestra is not kidding around anymore. They have aims. Glenn smiles at Vicky. That smile wouldn't fool anyone.

To play electric violin in a wedding orchestra you don't just need long fingers, you also need long hair, a long skinny black dress and long legs that can waltz around without looking at anything but the violin strings. To play guitar in a wedding orchestra you need to stay out of the violin's way, and also you need one of those faces. A face that is painfully empathic for what guitar strings are feeling. To be the keyboard person in a wedding orchestra you need to be able to smile at wedding guests for five hours straight and sing backup vocals. To be the drummer you need one of those heads that can survive the constant drubbing of invisible drumsticks and a neck not prone to whiplash. To sing lead vocals you need to know Farsi, English and Spanish, elementary Hebrew, and how to ad lib wedding-related lyrics without a hitch and when to pull the microphone off the microphone stand and unleash. To be any of these musicians or to be within seventy-five feet of them you need eardrums that like receiving little sonic explosions on a nonstop basis as long as you can dance to them, and nerves that can absorb a boom-boom-boom pulsing up from your feet before it stops your heart altogether and your chest caves in.

Before anyone knows what happened it's Israeli dance hour and people who normally have a little trouble walking are doing things on full stomachs that their cardiologists had never dreamed of warning them against. There is also a subtle change of demographics and the hora and other goings-around are piloted by the guys in beards and outfits that predate Dionne Warwick by one hundred years. They have been waiting for their turn. They are the guys who also decide it's time for the chair lift dance and that brides and grooms should have a little torture on their wedding night, just to keep things balanced.

Soon it's time for the band's first break and Michelle comes over looking a little irked about something and she and her mom and that lady Beverly get up from their table to go to the ladies room.

"Mom, do you know what your son did?" They're in the hallway going past the Century Room where the big Trombo fundraiser is happening.

Vicky asks "What?" She's not really listening.

"I feel a little guilty about being at the wrong dinner," says Beverly. They go into the ladies room. "It's a lovely wedding," she says, "but—" She leans over to make sure there are no feet, with ears, in any of the stalls. Then she turns toward Vicky. "I can't believe there are this many Iranians in the country." Now she starts thumbing in the direction of that fundraiser, outside and down the hall. "When he's President things will certainly turn back around."

"Mom, your son is crazy."

"Turn around how?" says Vicky to the mirror. Her lips are making that face for nothing. She recaps her lipstick almost as soon as she has it uncapped and ready. She's got Beverly's blonde hairdo in the foreground and her daughter's dark glare in the background. "Come on, let's not spoil our evening. I want to enjoy this party."

"Oh, I know you're related to the family, these are lovely people." She might be talking to the mirror or to the original, the two Vickys are hinged. "You're right, this is not a time for politics."

"Mom, tell Ryan to mind his own—"

"I will, I will, Honey."

Vicky blots her forehead with an ultrathick paper towel. Two of them could be a yoga mat. There are dozens in a stack on the counter and the stack has a special box. Teakwood is made for hotel bathrooms. Michelle is drying her hands. She throws the paper towel away but she looks like it was not an easy moral decision. She holds the door for Beverly, Beverly is holding it for Vicky. There's a moment of uncertainty. When they get back to their table Ryan is talking to his dad. He is telling his dad about a Persian wolf who was hitting on Michelle and thinks he's god's gift to women but he told the guy he didn't like his attitude toward women and the guy made a snooty face and walked off. Glenn is patting Ryan on the shoulder and Ryan is wistful as he stares at all the Persian girls wearing skin-tight dresses. Two of them walk by on their way to the soda table. The first one wears pink. The second one wears blue and walks five feet behind. Neither wears an expression.

Beverly says something to Vicky about seeing an electric violinist on that TV talent show and how wonderful she was, but she was Asian. Her husband Brian asks a catering staff member to take a picture of their table with his phone. Glenn and some of the other people have to stand up and get behind the people who can stay put. Glenn has pistachio skin in his teeth for the picture. Then one of the other couples wants a picture on their phone. Then one of the other couple's relatives from the next table wants a picture on their phone. Then two of Sheila's young co-workers come around and want to take pictures. Then Shadi comes around to greet everyone who came to her son's wedding and wants to take one of the whole table. Then Vicky takes Shadi's phone and takes one with Shadi in it. Then Beverly takes Shadi's phone and takes one with Shadi and Vicky in it. Then the wedding photographer comes and has to take their table and has to make half the people turn their chairs around. If anything is in Glenn's teeth it doesn't matter. He isn't smiling. He isn't even looking at the cameras. He's looking at his watch. And Vicky takes video.

The two girls walk by with their sodas. Pink, five feet of space, then blue. The sodas are probably good but they're not letting on.

The keyboardist is warming up and people are heading back to their tables and bringing seconds of some dishes and firsts of other dishes and the catering staff are working doubletime to collect dirty dishes and are accomplishing feats of crockery balancing that make you wonder why they were not put in charge of the chair lift dance.

After Vicky takes video of the centerpiece and the chandeliers and decorations and lights and the wedding party table and the less immediate wedding party table and the side of Glenn's face while he chews something she tells him that when the reception is over she wants the flowers. Nobody else at their table is close family, she says. Glenn seems untroubled by that.

The orchestra resumes and it's Persian pop music, which doesn't seem to require any lapse between songs, beautiful people are dancing Persian-style from one song straight into the next and even Michelle is out there doing the hands like everybody else. Half the crowd is singing along with the guy in the violet tuxedo and his voice that is only slightly louder than a jackhammer and Glenn is swaying or nodding depending on the piece. "What?" he says, shouting. He's on his third pair of earplugs tonight. This pair is really in there.

"I didn't say anything." Vicky says. She sips the refill of wine that she just brought back from the bar. Vicky isn't shouting. She's good at faces.

Beverly leans close to Vicky to tell her that she just thinks Senator Merrill is too liberal and that she's worried about this country going to the dogs. "With the gangs and the tattoos and the people getting welfare handouts?"

"No but what about our planet?" says Vicky. "What happens to your grandchildren with Trombo's coal factories and gas drilling and—"

"You know how much we pay in taxes every—" Brian quickly nudges his wife. She stops. He's looking around and then he points at something. It's young people taking group selfies while they're dancing. Beverly sits back in her chair. Vicky sits back in hers.

Glenn uses sign language and shouts "Restroom" and Vicky understands so he puts his hand on her bare shoulder as he gets up. He goes to the hotel lobby after the restroom and sits down in a deep chair where the back and the arms are one continuous oval. The chair is upholstered in brown vinyl, there are five others just like it. Next to Glenn's chair is one of the pillars that might hold up the ceiling of the lobby. The pillars are oval shape and covered with glossy bronze with ornaments hanging down, like long stringy baby crib mobiles.

He takes his earplugs out and sticks them in his suit pocket. Even here the music is plenty loud. There are a couple dozen other refugees from the wedding. Some people brought food out. Drinks. People are going outside to smoke or coming back in with fumes. A little kid with a bag of gummy worms wanders aimlessly and ends up in front of Glenn staring. She is eating a red one. Her dress is flouncy. She figures out how to put the red worm in the same hand that has the bag and finds a green one and holds it out for Glenn. Her mom is a few feet away and watching. The mom smiles.

Glenn looks at the mom. Then he looks at the little kid. He shakes his head. "No thank you, Sweetie. I'm on a low worm diet." Then he looks at the mom to see if she lives on the same lofty plane of humor as Glenn Stover. Based on her smile he may never be sure one way or the other. When he returns to the reception his earplugs are installed and he seems serious.

"Our whole planet'll suffer," Vicky is saying, not necessarily thinking of worms but possibly thinking of animal life in a broader sense. "We'll have droughts and famines and—oh hi, Honey."

Vicky's chair is at a strange angle. Glenn has a little trouble squeezing back into his seat. He smiles at everyone but has put himself on mute. He glances at Vicky's wine glass. It's a different color. Beverly wags a pale finger at Vicky to tell her that a professor from Pepperdine came to their church and the climate thing is just a false alarm.

"So what does your church say about Arthur Trombo and his history with women? Or his language. Every other word is—"

"Oh, that's just his way of letting off steam, he says he's a Christian and he'll ban all the abortions and let prayer back in schools instead of that evolution nonsense. And that's good enough for me."

Vicky has stopped listening and is pointing and asking Beverly and Brian to look at some little kids running between the tables with party favors. Vicky looks amused. And thirsty. Then another little kid runs past with two bags of party favors and through the blast of the music some little kid across the room is crying. "He must be a Trombo supporter," she says about the kid with the extra bag. She is taking video. She is in la-la land.

The two husbands glance at each other then look away quickly. Beverly puts her hand on Vicky's arm and starts to tell her what a devoted husband and father Arthur Trombo is. "I love his wife, she's so elegant."

Vicky expels a gust of air and laughter. "The Playpad Kitten? Mizz September of ninety-ninety?"

"Oh now, she was a child then, she's a very fine lady and she'll certainly dress up the White House. And—" Beverly's husband tries to get Vicky's attention and motions that she might want to video what's happening on the stage.

Glenn notices what the other guy is trying to do. "Look at Jason and Sheila, Honey," he says. "Can you believe that's little Jason?" The bride and groom are up with the band. They have the microphones and are screaming at the tops of their lungs and rocking out to some song that has something to do with getting knocked down and getting up again. They are having the time of their lives as Vicky grins and gets the rest of the performance on her phone. She's using the unsteady camera technique. Like some of those European art films.

Clattering dishes and novel food smells have everyone looking around about the time that the orchestra leader shuts the music down and introduces the Best Man. While people clap and whistle Glenn unstops his ears and puts the plugs away. The Best Man takes the mike and looks like a young Samuel L. Jackson and says he's Andrew and he met Jason in their freshman year at UC Davis. And immediately they were best friends. It was like they had known each other all their lives. Now it feels like they're brothers from another mother and he's got the crowd's humor lightly kindled. Glenn looks down and frowns at the eleven on his watch. He seems to blame it for where the hour hand has landed.

"What can I say about Jason?" Andrew doesn't take suggestions from the audience, he's probably just being rhetorical. "I could tell you about the time he got lost at the Homecoming Game and ended up in the Cal Poly section with his face painted green and gold. Or I could tell you about Jason's first fraternity party where he accidentally tipped over the punchbowl and almost got immediately voted out of the house. But all you really need to know about Jason is that he is the truest and kindest person you could ever hope to have as a friend."

"Wha a sweet tes'monial," Vicky says while she tries to keep the camera focused on the Best Man. He wraps up his speech and people clap and whistle and the orchestra guy takes the mike and introduces Sheila's married sister, the Matron of Honor, and people clap and whistle. "She so pretty," says Vicky. "Jus like Sheila."

"Sheila," says the Matron of Honor, holding the microphone in both hands, "I am so lucky to be your sister and you are my best friend in the world and now you have found the greatest guy in the world, which makes me so happy."

While she chokes up a little and blinks and tells Jason what a special person he is and that it's obvious he loves her sister more than anything in the world, Beverly leans close and whispers to Vicky that she thinks this sister is actually the prettier of the two. "She reminds me of Sigourney Trombo only not as striking. Did you see her debut, she was wonderful."

"I din see it."

"Well she's a beautiful actress."

"She's not, they say she so bad she could'n get a part inna dog food commercial if it wern for her husban."

Glenn's forefinger forms an instant perpendicular to his mouth. "Shshshshsh." He is sitting there red and clammy. He gets no acknowledgement from his own wife. But the other guy's wife gives him a look that Joan Crawford might have used in *Mildred Pierce* when she ends up betrayed by everyone. Glenn loosens his tie and opens the top button and looks up at the lights.

"—welcome you to the family with open arms. With that, please raise your glasses to toast the Bride and Groom. Jason and Sheila, we wish you both a lifetime of love, joy, and prosperity together. We love you from the bottom of our hearts. Cheers." She lifts her glass and so does the crowd and everyone claps and whistles, and claps and whistles again for Mrs. Yaghoubian the mother of the bride. Pretty and trim in the spotlight with the microphone, the mother looks more like another older sister. She starts out in Farsi, speaking softly. The crowd is very attentive. Even the Stovers are attentive. She must be a good cook, the mother, because the Farsi turns into a kind of spicy bilingual stew with random English words popping up and making the Americans look like they're not sure if they heard what they think they heard. Brian whispers to his wife that the word "celebration" must lack a suitable Farsi equivalent.

"Always," the mother concludes in scripted English, "what I want you remember, is I want you be happy, that is the most important thing and, what can I say, I always be there for you, and your future children."

She hands her husband the microphone so that they can share the sweet moment of ovation. The father of the bride looks a little old for the woman who just talked but he seems very comfortable holding a microphone and speaking in public. He also looks like he may have decided at some point that evening that he was entitled to a little liquid refreshment on the occasion of his daughter's marriage. "Your mother and I, we pray for you, we know you will follow Hashem in all your days and raise your children to believe as you believe and always do what the Torah says to do." After going on for longer than all the other speeches put together and in very formal English Mr. Yaghoubian stands at a table with a six foot egg challah and does the hamotzi.

"L'Chaim," says Vicky with her wine glass as everyone else is silent. The father starts slicing the challah. Glenn keeps checking his watch and looking around like he's expecting people to start banging their butter knives on their tables and chanting "Dinner, dinner". Servers bring trays of sliced challah around. And then dinner is announced. Twenty minutes to twelve.

Brian and Beverly stand up. Brian doesn't say "after you" but he stops next to the Stovers and extends his hand toward the main buffet area.

"I think we'll wait til things thin out a little bit," Glenn says. The other couple doesn't stay and argue, they move on toward the smells of a thousand spices. The girl in pink goes by on her way to the buffet. Then her friend in blue. Their walk, their spacing, their faces are as unchanging as stone.

"Dear," says Beverly when she and her husband get back with full plates of meat, rice and stews, "you mustn't judge someone if you haven't even seen their work. Now if—"

"Mus'n I? You mean Trombo's trophy wife? Say, thas pretty good, Trombo's trophy wife."

"She's certainly not a trophy wife, she is a talented actress, my husband knows talent, after all he's with Pyramid Pictures."

"Well my husban wuzza bes felony D.A. in town, he won more verdicts'n anyone, an he duzzen need any a you fancy Hollywood people an your stupid Oscars."

She throws her arms around Glenn's neck and starts kissing him all over his face and neck. He struggles to stand up with his wife hanging on. "All right, Sweetheart. I think we're ready to say goodnight to all these nice people."

"Rilly? So early?"

"I think we've had enough fun for one night." He waves Ryan over.

"What's wrong with Mom?"

"I think we're gonna have to hit the road."

"We haven't had dinner." He looks back at his plate.

"You kids eat and Mom and I will wait in the lobby." He starts to walk Vicky toward the exit.

"My centerpiece," she says, looking up at Glenn like a little girl who left her dolly in a park. The catering staff are collecting abandoned or dirty dishes. People are going back for seconds of chicken kabob. The very enterprising are gathering one of everything from the dessert tables. The girl in pink and the girl in blue are sitting at their table watching and giggling together.

His kids have to listen to all his calculations out loud. "The hotel alone probably cost eighty grand, without the catering. Which was kosher." He puts a price tag on the whole enchilada.

"That much, Dad? I could buy a house for that."

"Not around here," Michelle says.

"I mean someplace normal. Like Seattle." For a few seconds Ryan drives with one hand, the way people are socialized yawning takes priority over other things, like driving. Even if they're the only person in the car. That might explain some traffic mishap statistics. His eyes are moist and he is still blinking but Ryan has two hands on the wheel again.

"If we're lucky, Dad, she won't remember very much of tonight." In the back seat Michelle tries to see her mom's eyes. Vicky's head is propped on her daughter's shoulder. There's a little tributary of mascara dried up along one nostril. "She looks so innocent when she's asleep. Why does she keep mumbling something about dog food commercials?"

"We had Iranian food," says Ryan, "but my mouth tastes like Chinese food."

Glenn smacks his lips. "Mine tastes like Indian."

Michelle wants to know if anyone feels like ice cream.

"Everything is closed," Ryan says.

Glenn is looking at the dashboard clock. "I thought it was an hour later than it is."

Ryan says he's glad it's not an hour later than it is. "Because if it's an hour later than it is—I don't know what I'm saying, I'm so tired." The young man grips the steering wheel tight and stares straight into the dark red-sequined party dress that the 405 North becomes late at night.

"Isn't that the same car that—" His dad is pointing at a large speeding object.

SIXTEEN

S he's a good girl. She hears it thirty-five or forty times a day in a warm male voice, so it's sunk in. She's mellow. She's been around the block. She doesn't pull at the leash. Her grandpa is her biggest fan. Their afternoon walk along the green belt has become a highlight of his day. They know four other dogs and dog owners by name. One says he's a purebred. The guy's dog has a pretty good pedigree too, he says. Glenn likes this guy.

Today they're staying in the shady part of the green belt. Claudia pants a lot in the sun. Glenn stops and gives her some water in a little bowl hooked to her leash. This part of the green belt is the part by the school and the baseball field. There's a game going on with eight or nine year olds. The Orioles versus the Titans. Some parents are on the sidelines and in the bleachers. A couple coaches are talking it up. Stuff like "Good eye". "Let's see some hustle out there." "Ya gotta make those plays, Lucas."

Glenn and Claudia stand behind home plate and watch the game through the high chain-link fence. Glenn

129

is smiling. He pushes his sunglasses up his nose. Claudia lies down on the concrete and pants. One kid takes a base on balls and takes a pretty good lead off of first base and then starts inching back toward the base while the Oriole pitcher takes his cap off and wipes his forehead with his sleeve and puts the cap on and looks around at the infield. The next kid comes up to bat and spits and takes three or four mighty practice swings. He adjusts the sweat bands on his wrists. He takes his stance. The kid's chest says Titans but his back says Rollie's Pizza. He grimaces at the pitcher, his braces twinkle in the sun. The coaches are clapping their hands and bombarding their teams with chatter.

There's the pitch, a swing and a hit. Bounces past the shortstop and into center field. The kid discards his bat and races to first base, the runner on first rounds second and slides into third. Glenn pounds his fist in the air, exuberant.

Suddenly the Oriole coach standing behind the catcher and the umpire picks up the bat and hurls it backwards with all his strength along with an angry strand of words that aren't allowed in school or in baseball. It's a hard metal bat, it slams into the dirt and bounces against the fence where Glenn is watching. Gut reflexes don't see chain-link, they just see hurtling objects. Claudia yelps and cowers next to Glenn and Glenn flinches and ducks. Then the former benchwarmer who was happy if they even put him in for an inning stiffens and glares. He grabs the fence with all his fingers and puts his flushed face right up to it. "Hey! Is there a problem?"

The guy may or may not have heard.

"Hey is there a problem?"

"Yeah." The guy's a tall athletic type with premature gray hair. He looks straight at Glenn. "My team."

With a frown and shaking his head, Glenn turns. He walks Claudia farther along the green belt away from the school. When they get to the three ancient cottonwoods

Glenn looks up. "That's the last person in the world who should be coaching kids," he says, "what kind of example is that?" The old prosecutor vents, three lofty green heads listen and nod. "These are kids! It's a game! Lighten up! Kids need to know it's okay to make mistakes. Baseball should be fun, not a jury trial. They need to learn sportsmanship. Sportsmanship!" Claudia looks at Glenn like this might be some kind of new game. Twenty yards up the path a little cottontail rabbit is playing statue. "The catcher was five feet away, the bat could have taken a bad bounce and wiped the kid out!" At this ugly image the trees throw up their arms, they shudder and moan.

When they get to the place where the green belt ends and regular streets and houses begin, a guy with a middle-aged mustache and two big dogs is approaching down the sidewalk. They're one of those pointy breeds, the one with teeth like Dracula and you never want to make eye contact with even though you know their eyes are on you like you're a choice T-bone at feeding time. Glenn watches as the guy approaches with his pulling dogs. The guy is trying to hold the dogs back and little by little is shortening both leashes by turning his wrists and wrapping them around and around his forearms.

Glenn gathers up the slack of Claudia's leash and has her over on the grass by the time the two dogs pass, snuffling and straining. "Now what is this guy trying to prove?" he says. He scowls down at Claudia. "Let's go back, girl."

When they get back to the part of the path that skirts the schoolyard the bleachers are emptying out and folks are packing their gear. Glenn stops and stares at a small sedan parked in one of the handicapped spots nearby. The guy who threw the bat is sitting sideways in the passenger seat, changing his shoes on the curb. He's changing from some kind of cleats to some kind of street shoes. The feet and ankles sticking out of his sweatpants are the kind that don't have feet or ankles and are custom-made out of fiberglass if you want to run or do sports after you come home from the Middle East and go through rehab and get your head together.

There's a pretty woman getting into the driver's side, and the kids are in the back. Even from where Glenn stands it's pretty obvious from the arms sticking out of the windows that, if this is a family, it's the kind of family that evolved less from biology and more from Family Court and the adoption statutes of the State of California.

Glenn and Claudia head quietly for home.

If Trombo doesn't stop interrupting and the moderator doesn't do something Senator Merrill looks like she might go offstage and get her handbag to see if she has any duct tape. Trombo is heckling her with his loud baritone and it's obvious he hopes to rattle her to the point of desperation. He flings interjections like "bull pucky" and "cry me a river" whenever she starts sounding presidential and scoring points with the audience.

The audience in the Elliott Hall of Music in West Lafayette looks like it's basketball season and Purdue is down thirty points to IU at halftime and their center is riding the bench with four fouls. They are quiet and blue.

Senator Merrill looks really pretty in blue, with a flowered scarf tucked at the throat of her nice navy suit. She has only lost her cool once so far, and that was only to interrupt and tell Trombo he's profoundly misinformed, he's never even seen the inside of a public school classroom. The moderator gave Trombo fifteen extra seconds, but she's had to give Senator Merrill extra seconds twelve times already. And they haven't even gotten to the economy yet.

Vicky hasn't looked at her phone for twenty minutes. She is draped with Aunt Phyllis' afghan and bristling at the TV when Glenn comes back from closing the upstairs windows to keep the rain out that wasn't supposed to get here until the weekend. He's holding his cell phone. It shouldn't take ten minutes to close three windows.

He sits on the couch. He's a more mysterious person than can be explained by the network broadcast of a presidential debate or an early rain. Vicky looks at her unreadable husband who is normally an open book.

"Did you leave the bathroom window open?" she says.

He takes the remote and turns down the TV. "I had a voicemail. I didn't know I had it." He tells her that someone who is a Casting Director says they're interested in him. They would like him to audition for a supporting part in a feature film. The audition is in two weeks. Apparently, it all has something to do with some outtake footage of him from one of the studio cameras that was shooting the courtroom scene a couple months ago. One of the Assistant Directors saved the footage on a whim.

Glenn is dismissive of the crazy idea but Vicky encourages him to at least check it out.

"It can't hurt," she says.

Glenn isn't too enthusiastic. He changes the subject to dinner.

"I thought you were warming up the pasta," she says.

"I was but I think I'll have a salad. Want some?"

He wouldn't be in those pants if he hadn't been riding workout machines for the past week and a half. He's not riding anything at the moment. But he's blowing out air like fifteen minutes on his Reclino-Cycle.

"Slate?" he says.

"Yeah, just say your name and the part you're reading for."

Glenn says it.

"Now say it to the camera. Then whenever you're ready." The casting director uses her head to point to her left. Otherwise she rests her mouth on her fingertips. They're painted pink and they're collaborating in a nice pose. If she closed her eyes and said God bless Mother and Uncle Stewie and Billy and Scruffy it would make a nice scene. The camera guy is smiling at Glenn. Maybe Glenn reminds him of his grandfather, before the broken hip.

Glenn turns to the camera and with enlarged eyes repeats his slate. He swallows and glances at the reader long enough for any reader to infer a green light.

"Mr. Filmore," says the reader in a voice that would like to be sterner, but already has an acting job, "I am expecting you to impress upon your clients the gravity of their situation."

"Yes, Your Honor," says Glenn too loud and gravelly. He says it to the reader and he watches the reader reading along. Glenn stands next to a wooden chair with a straight back. On the chair is a highlighted script with damp thumbmarks along the edges. This is not a big room, it would make a nice TV room in a basement. Two walls are brick and they're painted the color of hummus. Garbanzo-colored bricks are behind Glenn and off to his right. The casting people sit behind a long low table either spellbound or thinking about flavored coffee drinks. They don't seem to think the room is unusually warm. "I've advised them that the Court has been more than generous in its disposition of their case, and that they should be very grateful that they are not being remanded forthwith to the hospitality of Sheriff Barnes." Glenn looks taller than he did ten seconds ago. His throat has done a nice job resurfacing its asphalt.

"I don't want to hear you putting fancy words in your clients' mouths, Mr. Filmore, about how grateful they are. I want you to tell me that you're going to kick their little designer butts from Rodeo Drive to Central Avenue if they don't do every single hour of their community service and do it with a smile."

"I hear you plain and clear, Your Honor, and I wear size eleven and a half wing tips." Casting folks are pros, they can chuckle inwardly since everything is recorded.

"Mr. Filmore, you just lighted up my docket for the first time this week. Congratulations. Now I've got one to tell my husband when I get home. You and your pretty little sticky-fingered clients are excused. That'll be the order. Off the record. Oh, Mr. Filmore?"

"Sorry, Your Honor?"

"Approach the bench, will you?"

"No problem, Your Honor."

"Now, you know as well as I do that you've got three spoiled narcissists for clients. As you can see, I hand-picked their community service assignments because I need them to reflect upon their behavior in light of what's out there in the real world. You know what I'm talking about. You've been doing this for as long as I have. Maybe longer."

"Definitely longer. But it's always a pleasure being in your Court, Your Honor. You've always been eminently fair with my clients. I think your order in this case is brilliant."

"Well don't lay it on too thick, Mr. Filmore. By the way, Ms. Campos was licking her lips the whole time I was reading the order. Like she couldn't feel them."

Glenn turns and looks back at the brick wall, then goes back to staring at the reader. "She had work done on her face, Your Honor, and I don't pretend to understand why women think they have to do that to themselves."

"She looks like Jake LaMotta slapped her across the mouth forty or fifty times. I imagine she'd be quite pretty if she had left her face alone."

"I could tell her something but I'm afraid it goes a little beyond legal advice."

"No, just advise Ms. Van Winkle to wear something a little more modest next time she comes to court. I could almost see her—uh, you're excused, Mr. Filmore."

Glenn grins, then holds the grin until the Casting Director says "Very nice. You seemed very comfortable playing a lawyer. So you'll hear something within a week. Thank you so much for coming in."

"Nice meeting you all," says Glenn. In the outer room half a dozen people are sitting with highlighted scripts or checking emails. Two of them look like middle-aged lawyers.

It has his picture on the cover. It probably sold eighty thousand copies the first day. Every once in a while Glenn closes the book with his right thumb still in it and looks at the cover for a minute or so. He squints. Nobody has ever asked Glenn why he squints so much even when there's no sun in his eyes. Clint Eastwood is squinting too, on the cover, but neither of these two guys needs to squint right now since the sun won't come in through the sliding glass door and hit the top of Glenn's recliner-rocker for another hour and a half.

Glenn might have stayed in his recliner-rocker for the entire hour and a half if it hadn't been for the funny sound. It's coming from the back yard. Glenn lowers the footrest and gets up and goes to the screen door where the air is warm. He squints through the mesh. She is crying, she is sniffling. There are also little sounds in her throat from time to time. Her little vocal folds are wrung with emotion.

He puts on his sandals and goes out and sits in the patio chair next to her chair, under the umbrella. He can put his arm around her but it's not easy in patio chairs. He says "What, Honey?" but his face is not expecting an answer. He looks where she is looking. There's a little bird eating on the ground where she puts birdseed in decorative objects that are part of her garden. He tries to get her to tell him what it's all about, she just shakes her head.

Glenn watches the little bird until it flies up into the bushes. With his handkerchief he has to dab his eyes a little bit where they are squinting and watering. He puts his handkerchief hand on his knees, which the umbrella can't shade at this time of day. They are not turning red yet. They'll need another ten minutes of noon sun. They are not very white next to the handkerchief but next to the brown of his corduroy shorts they are. Two of the neighbors' dogs are barking, sporadically. They're big. Somewhere beyond the neighbors' yard a leaf blower whirrs. From her side of the dividing wall Claudia is barking back, and otherwise sniffing through Vicky's flowers and shrubs. Claudia and the neighbors' dogs have never actually seen each other.

Once the blower shuts off the dogs snuff a few times and settle down. "The dove was here."

He looks at her profile. "Oh."

"He wasn't really eating, he, he was looking at me." Vicky's throat is still a cradle of emotion, she says she started talking to the dove, she told him how pretty he is and how much they like him. "He was really looking at me, really listening. He had his head cocked, you know, like a little terrier. He really listened for a long time. Then I stopped talking and then he walked over there and then he flew away." She tells Glenn it was the most touching thing she's ever seen. "I couldn't help it, the tears just came."

"It's okay, Sweetheart, you're entitled."

"I'm off my meds."

"That'll do it."

"I didn't have my phone, I might have taken video. But it was better this way."

"How do you know it's not a she?"

"I can't tell."

"No. I guess they can. What about the Scrub Jays?" One just swooped down to grab as many sunflower seeds as it can carry in its beak.

"They're all beautiful. To our eyes."

"I think this is a male. Look how greedy he is."

"The Trombo of the bird world."

Glenn smiles. "Only smarter."

"And that squawk. When I think of the dove and how much I love her song, the prettiest sound in all of—"

He holds out his handkerchief and she takes it. This isn't a time to be fussy.

SEVENTEEN

He got Glenn a diet soda before they went into his office which is off the kitchen which is bigger than Glenn and Vicky's living room. He isn't sitting at his desk that was imported from somewhere equatorial, he is sitting at one end of the couch and Glenn at the other. They're both wearing comfortable shoes but only Glenn is wearing socks. He is filling Glenn in on some of the social and psychological themes behind his concept.

"I have a pretty big part, Stan," Glenn says. When he says it he can look out the window and see the water next to Paradise Cove and is close enough to count the waves. If he and Stan turned around they could see some of the hills that nobody in Malibu ever thought houses could be built on but they were wrong. Right now nobody knows if fires will come to the hills again before floods do or the other way around, and they would be right.

"You do," Stan says. "You're the *nexus*, as you lawyers put it."

"Law school?"

Stan shakes his head. "*Casey Littlefield, Public Counsel.* I directed Seasons Two and Three."

"I don't watch lawyer shows."

"Neither do I."

Glenn tells Stan that he really likes the phone call scene where he has to beg his wife to come down and bail him out on Contempt of Court charges. "Where Harry Filmore has to beg his wife, I mean—"

"No, no, that's okay," Stan says. "It's good that you've become your character. You're starting to internalize the role. You are Harry Filmore."

"I guess I'm doing the Method. Heh."

When he smiles Stan Elway still looks like a Director but not the kind that can afford to live in Malibu.

"I also like the scene where Danielle confesses to me about her gambling addiction. Very realistic. But I'm a little nervous about the one where Kimberly makes a pass at me to make her fiancé jealous. The kissing and hair mussing and everything. I haven't kissed another woman since 1981. Besides my wife, I mean."

"That's okay, Glenn. Use those nerves as a positive. Even good old dependable Harry is entitled to a case of nerves, isn't he? You'll be great, I guarantee it."

"Ah." He takes a couple sips of soda and glances up at one of Stan's framed movie posters of his previous projects. This one was the picture about the woman who woke up one day and could see what everybody will be doing and what they will look like on the day before they die. Glenn has seen little bits of it on TV four times.

"And how about getting to play a hot tub scene with Sigourney Trombo, the most beautiful Playpad Kitten ever and possibly our next First Lady. Pretty exciting, huh? Have you two met yet?"

They haven't, Glenn says. He swallows.

"I'll talk to Barb, the Production Coordinator, and set up a meeting. What's a good time for you?" Stan touches things on his cell phone and puts it to his ear.

From where he is sitting the woman in the poster seems to be looking at Glenn and seeing things that aren't in any script yet and if they were might require some major special effects.

It's dark in the booth and Glenn hasn't even tried to read the menu. The menu is almost as heavy as the shooting script of "The Universe and Other Responsibilities" that Director Stan Elway gave him in a loose leaf binder with his name on it. Glenn says he always wanted to try this place. He keeps looking up at all the black and white photos of movie stars even though sitting right under them just eighteen inches away and drinking tea and smiling is an ex-Playpad Kitten and possible First Lady dressed more like her past than her future.

"George Brent," says Glenn, indicating with his head. "He was so great in The Spiral Staircase."

"Oh, I never saw it. That was before my time."

It's a little dark to see the face of a middle aged lawyer prove the theory of gravity. "Uh, what kind of movies do you and your husband watch, Mrs. Trombo?"

"Call me Sigourney. No formality between fellow actors. Ha ha."

"You said you've been here many times. I guess you and your husband get out to California quite a bit

"No, just me."

"Mmmmh. I can't read this."

"I know the menu forwards and backwards. I'll order something really special for you." She pats his hand. Two pats. They're seated at right angles, her arm could have measured the hypotenuse if it weren't for the soy sauce.

Glenn says well, that's fine but it's his treat. She just laughs. Another two pats. Glenn retracts his hand and covers a cough that looks fake, there's no casting director here. He flicks a quick glance over his shoulder at the bar area. Then he says something about a case he once had where the defendant only robbed Japanese steakhouses and always demanded takeout for two along with the till and she starts to tell him how she dated a lawyer once and he talked like he was reciting the Declaration of Independence and she only understood about two words. There are two young guys in the next booth and the one who is closest to Glenn's lunch companion is resting his head back, inhaling deeply, and revolving his empty cup as if green tea were catnip for second year film students.

There's a woman at the bar drinking Irish beer on draft. There are seven large and medium men posted in and around the restaurant to guard a body. It is hard to say if Mrs. Trombo's body acts like it is being guarded or not.

The woman at the bar drinking Irish beer on draft mostly swivels her barstool away from the bar so that she can rest her back against the round knobby edge of it. She looks at Glenn and his fellow thespian. Besides beer her lunch is pretzel, cereal and nut mix basted with MSG. She can't stop munching. It's a mix that is very prominent and also probably accounts for ten to twelve percent of North American beer sales. Pretty soon the woman takes out her phone and starts to video Glenn and Mrs. Trombo. They just got their Wonton Soup. The woman moves a couple barstools over to get closer and a better camera angle. She seems to have one of those phones with upgraded storage. One of the seven men comes over and stands in front of her camera.

"Can I ask what you're photographing there?"

"You at the moment, young man. Do you mind moving?"

He wants to know why he should hafta move and claims a legal right to stand here. By the way they're hoisted, the man's eyebrows seem pretty sure that push comes to shove he's on solid ground, constitutionally-speaking.

"Fine. I'll move." She grabs her purse and goes to an empty booth. The man's right to stand seems portable and weirdly tethered to Vicky and her phone. Like a pesky chess piece he moves for the block. Vicky's new view would have been a nice close-up of her husband and Mrs. Trombo, their chopsticks and their Shrimp Mu Shu. But it's a guy who probably picked out his own cologne and doesn't know how much is ample. The guy is wearing Glenn's good trial suit, only from the big and tall rack. Vicky says something about starting to get ticked off and flexes her thin shoulders around and says that cheap bar snacks for lunch didn't help her mood any so the guy signals for backup and talks to Vicky for a minute about people having the right to live their lives in peace and have their privacy respected.

"What if I'm a journalist?" She hiccups.

"For who?"

"I'm just asking, what if I'm a journalist?"

It's still an invasion of privacy, according to the bodyguard, and he wants to know who she is or at least what she's really doing there. She looks at him. Then she looks at his backup on either side of her. Those two guys and the first guy probably don't do sleepovers at each other's houses and might not borrow each other's suits but they probably could if they wanted to just for fun and variety. They look like fun and variety in their world is mostly found in pizza toppings and cable sports channels.

Thirty seconds later she is seated next to Glenn. "I didn't know she was your wife, Sir. If she had only said something right off the bat." Glenn tells the man it's okay and while the three faces in the booth are as red and steamy as the peppers in the Kung Pao chicken, the waiter comes over and asks if they'll be needing another place setting or ordering additional items. Sigourney flails Glenn on the shoulder with her napkin.

"Glenn. How could you leave your sweet wife at the bar while you and I are sitting here with a six course meal?" It's a gentle flailing.

"Oh, I don't know, it was, I mean, she didn't really feel—"

"I am so embarrassed. Of course I want to meet your lovely wife. You are so pretty, Mrs. Stover, have you been in pictures too?" She slides the Sichuan Eggplant, the Whitefish Dumplings and the Honey Glaze Walnut Shrimp all to Vicky's side of the table.

Vicky shakes her head. "Well, I was an extra on Hall of Justice. Huh. Oh this looks wonderful."

"Glenn, you didn't tell me that your wife is an actress in her own right."

"Uh—"

"I would love to see your work, Vicky. You have that Sally Field kind of aura."

"Oh, my. I've been wanting to see your other movie but I, well we never had a chance." Nervous smile.

"Flying Ego wasn't very good," says Sigourney. "It was my debut."

"Oh, I'm sure you were great. Everybody said so."

Glenn is passing Vicky the Braised Pork Belly but stops.

"They did? Say, who's your favorite all-time actress?"

Vicky tells Mrs. Trombo that she's always thought that there was something special about Doris Day that no other actress ever had. "Present company excepted, Mrs. Trombo."

Mrs. Trombo thinks the last little qualifier is funny and says she wishes she had half the talent of Doris Day's little finger and that Vicky should call her Sigourney. And Vicky calls her that and asks her the same question and Sigourney picks a lo mein noodle off the low-cut part of her sweater, puts it on her fork and slurps it, and says either Doris Day or Goldie Hawn.

Mrs. Trombo is softhearted and asks Vicky if she can't finish that last potsticker. Glenn has been eyeing it since the waiter took away the empty plates of everything else including the crispy noodles.

"I'm stuffed. You're sure you don't—"

Mrs. Trombo shakes her head.

"I hate to see it go to waste," Vicky says. Glenn watches his wife make two bites with her fork and demonstrate that they don't stick to mouths.

The waiter brings fortune cookies, orange slices and more tea. Glenn pours. They do the fortune cookies. Glenn is about to embark on a new adventure. Sigourney claps her hands and says it's true, he already is. She cracks her cookie and won't eat it and nobody else wants it. A long journey awaits her and she blushes. Vicky looks at Glenn and takes out her reading glasses. She is loyal and trustworthy and will be rewarded by lifelong friendship. She smooths the wrinkles of her fortune on the tabletop. Both women drink their tea.

Lawyers are trained in diplomacy. They also like getting to the truth by sweet-talking people into spilling their guts. Glenn gets Sigourney to talk a little about her husband and his political philosophy and how he ended up jumping into the race for President without any previous public service. She's pretty crazy about the guy, it shows in everything she says about him, she's just not too keen on the campaigning and the protests and the terrible things that people write about his past and his family and his friends and his character. He's been called so many things and a lot of the things he's been called she's never even heard of but they sound bad.

"So that's why you're not going on a "long journey" with your husband's campaign and you're doing this movie instead?"

"See, Vicky. You get me. Nobody else gets me. Arthur's kids hate me for not supporting him. I support him totally, but politics is, I just, it's just not for me, I don't like it."

"Um," says Glenn, taking the check from the waiter, glancing at it and swallowing, "do you think any of these things that are said about him could possibly be just a little bit true?"

She shakes her head and her eyes are almond cookies, without the cellophane. "Only they call him a rich opportunist, and he is rich. We can't say he's not. But what's that got to do with anything? They say he's right-wing but everybody's right or left or somewhere. It's very unfair. He's a wonderful husband and father, he's a fantastic businessman, salesman, importer and exporter. Look what he's built for himself, think what he could do for the rest of the country."

"Sigourney," says Vicky, "look how eloquent you are. You would do great on the campaign trail."

"Not in public, with thousands of people."

"Sure, they're just people. If you believe strongly in what you say, the words will just come out by themselves."

"Vick, if she doesn't like politics she doesn't like it. Don't force her."

"I'm not, Dear, I'm just—"

"Also she's in the middle of shooting a movie, which is her own career, which is just as important as—"

"I'm so glad I met you two. You're both so sweet and supportive. That's what I really need right now." The First Lady candidate is looking into the ambiance of the room like she's never seen a red paper lantern before. She's twisting her wedding ring around the photogenic finger that has modeled it for nine years. The diamond looks like Vicky's except it looks like Vicky's if it were being studied under a magnifying glass. "I wish we could have dinner like this every night."

What's written in the looks that telegraph between wives and their husbands could sometimes fill a book, or at least a restaurant napkin or two.

Before they all leave Vicky apologizes to the bodyguards, no hard feelings, just doing their job. "Glad you guys are here to protect Mrs. T., please keep her safe, there are a lot of crazy people around."

EIGHTEEN

The producers and writers and studio honchos won't sit at the table. They'll have to sit in a row of chairs by the wall, the one that's mostly a big long window that people can gawk through if they're not playing with their phones when they walk past the conference room. The table is shaped like a Hawaiian yam and there are about thirty chairs around it and printed name placards at each place. Glenn's has his full name and just "Harry" for his character. Glenn looks at his complimentary water bottle. It's West Coast Studios Water according to the label with its logo that movie fans have become familiar with lately at the multiplexes. Sometimes Glenn's face doesn't smile but wants to. He puts the bottle down within arm's reach. He puts it down behind his copy of the REVISED SCRIPT that has his name at the top and today's date. There's a red pen. The cap is hard to get off.

A couple people who act like production assistants and a couple people who act like actors are the only ones who managed to beat Glenn to the table reading. Some more show up and there are some friendly ones who like to meet people and be met at the first chance they get so pretty soon Glenn is friends with everyone and makes one or two corny comments that are the sure-fire kind for groups who just met. There doesn't seem to be any question of everyone liking Glenn. Stan the Director is there in time to join the fun talk and some munching on studio snacks that comes before the table reading. Nobody is standing on ceremony.

Stan's First Assistant Director rounds everybody up and herds them to their places at the table. She has management skills but she's also tall and has bone structure and Glenn looks at her like she oughta be in pictures, if not the sequel to Cattle Drive then maybe this one. Sometimes they'd rather be behind the camera and just be Marilyn the First AD instead of stardom.

Glenn pages through scenes. There are eleven conversations around the table and also across it at odd angles. They whistle past Glenn's ears like bullets through a surrounded wagon train.

"That was a night shoot. Because I think they had a six p.m. call time."

"There's only so much I can do."

"I've never done that before but it seems to work."

"I was roller skating in the lobby."

"It goes all the way down."

"You gotta do it like within seconds."

"I guess they sent it to production and they accepted it"

"The craziest."

"Yeah. Exactly a year."

"Early, and ready, and dressed right."

"It's a different name now, it used to be Guadalupe's."

"A quota thing, you know."

"So I thought should I, should I not."

"I just drink one beer and I stop."

"No that was the other Fred Thompson."

A hand descends on Glenn's shoulder and becomes a vice. The hand has tattoos and heavy steel bracelets. He says there she is his fairy godmother. He says he was hoping she would be here and for Glenn that's as neon a smile as can be switched on by other than dogs or dead composers.

Sierra the Second AD says she would have to lose a shitload of piercings and put on a frickin dress to qualify for a fairy godmother's wand. Her hair isn't green anymore it's some color between brown and black that might occur somewhere in nature but not on heads.

"I hope I don't let you down," Glenn says.

"Dude, you're gonna rock this frickin script."

"When you guys called about the audition I was in shock, I, I didn't really have a chance to say how much I—"

"Dude, that frickin outtake was the most outrageous thing I'd seen since I got sober. When you stood up and told the judge 'I object'," she says in a deep voice, "'that calls for bullshit.' I could've wet my boxers."

"I don't think I stood up."

"Whatever, Glenn, it was brilliant. Now kick their asses across this table."

Stan's seat is the head of the table. He looks at his watch and at Marilyn the First AD and Marilyn looks at her phone and back at Stan again. They both look down the elliptical table at their elliptical cast. They have about a minute and a half to work on those actions. Before Sigourney Trombo finally arrives. Mrs. Trombo's bodyguards station themselves outside by the door and along the window wall. She hugs Stan and Marilyn and the Producer and the Writer and a few other people. Marilyn guides her to her seat. Sigourney sees Glenn sitting across the table, squeals and runs around the table with her name placard. She blushes and with a voice like local honey apologizes to the whole bunch who have to shift their seats so that she can sit next to Glenn. Nobody

151

seems to mind and everyone, even the veteran actors, are beaming and flushing on the chance that she will notice them and smile their way. Glenn is halfway to purple. He gets a hug he won't soon forget.

There's an expression that First AD's wear. It's when studio timetables and protocols are flaunted. Marilyn does it so well she probably should do a headshot.

It's a long table. Stan tugs a little at all the tight places of his sweater vest. He gives his opening pep talk standing. It's kind of like an Oscar speech only forward-looking. He's excited to have this cast and crew, he's fanatic about the script, he's grateful to all the production companies, he knows they've got a hit on their hands and he can't wait to get started. He gets started. They go around the table and everybody says their name and the character they're playing. A couple people add something funny. Even Glenn says "and I play Harry Filmore, an honest lawyer" and gets a laugh. Stan is the person who is going to read the stage directions. It's a good thing he decided to go into directing.

"Fade In," he says. "Interior Andrea's bedroom. Day. With hip-hop music and video pouring from her phone, we open on a young, beautiful woman, Andrea, getting dressed in a classy business suit, doing her hair and makeup and grabbing a quick breakfast before dashing out of the house as the hip-hop music fades out. Interior Danielle's bathroom. Day. Serene classical music fades in as we see Danielle, another beautiful young woman, shaving her legs luxuriously in the bath. She is smiling and humming and occasionally using her razor as a baton to direct the orchestra. The classical music fades out as she finishes shaving, gently splashes herself with water and turns on the tap and enveloping steam starts rising from the tub. Interior Kimberly's kitchen. Day. A telephone is ringing and Kimberly, a beautiful young woman dressed in a tight low-cut dress, switches off a TV in the middle of a morning talk show and answers the phone." Stan looks up and smiles in the direction of Sigourney. She is underlining lines in her script.

"Hi, Mr. Filmore," she says with her red pen gripped tight. She is blushing. "Yes, I should be there by ten."

Stan reads again. "Kimberly hangs up and calmly takes a moment to inspect her beautiful nails before sauntering away. Interior Harry's car. Day. Harry, a middle-aged lawyer in a conservative dark suit, is driving on Santa Monica Boulevard in Beverly Hills. He is driving with one hand and talking on his cell phone. He looks a little nervous." Stan glances over at Glenn.

"Good-bye," says Glenn. His voice is hoarse. Sigourney squeezes Glenn's arm. She is quivering with excitement.

"Harry puts down his phone just in time to brake suddenly for a red light," says Stan. "His briefcase slides off the passenger seat. It's a nice briefcase but apparently wasn't closed properly because papers and files spill out onto the floor. Harry looks sadly at the mess, until the car behind him starts honking. The light is green."

By Scene 22 everybody has settled down and almost everybody around the table has had lines to read and everybody did fine with some going full out with gestures and high volume and others holding back and being understated with the obvious implication that both of those groups believe that their way of doing table readings is a sign of true confidence. Marilyn is the only person who hasn't settled down and has circled the table extensively because she wants to make sure that anyone who wants extra water or pens or highlighters or loses their place in the script gets whatever intervention they need so that the reading goes smoothly and they can get a pretty good idea of how the whole thing flows and the approximate running time.

"Interior coffee shop. Day," says Stan. "Danielle and Harry are in line at a gourmet coffee shop. Harry has his wallet out. Danielle is ordering."

"Whole wheat bagel," says the actress who plays Danielle, "lightly toasted, low-fat cream cheese on the side. Raspberry cappuccino with shaved dark chocolate on top. Shaved, not powdered."

"Small coffee and one of those bagels," says Glenn.

"They find a small table in the corner and their conversation takes place while they have their bagels and coffee." Stan turns to the next page of script, then turns back.

"Two hundred hours of community service is cruel and unusual punishment, Harry." She reads it serious. She smiles at her neighbors. Everyone wants to follow along with the script but it's fun to look around and watch everybody reading their lines.

"Harry looks skeptically at Danielle," says Stan.

"I was pre-law at USC," she says. "I've done eighteen horrendous hours, that should be enough."

"Danielle, your attitude is not what Judge Avery had in mind," says Glenn. "You're not taking all this in the right spirit. You're not accepting responsibility. You're not showing remorse." Glenn swallows. His face has the cloud of someone who feels he is being watched. He slowly turns his head to the right. Mrs. Trombo is gazing at him starstruck.

"It's disgusting there. I almost threw up. But what's worse, it's depressing. I don't need to see that stuff."

Glenn's eyes are back on his script. "The Court thinks you do."

"I'm having nightmares."

"You can practice doing makeup on the women in the shelter, think of it as a challenge, think how it will feel to take something ugly and disgusting and make it gorgeous. Think of it as a modern-day Pygmalion."

"I played Eliza Doolittle in my high school musical."

"There you go. The Judge will love the cosmic justice, a Beverly Hills brat who shoplifts high-priced makeup and pays her debt to society by doing makeovers on homeless women on skid row."

"Oh, god. I suppose. Can you get the judge to knock off a hundred hours?"

"I'll buy you another cappuccino."

"You better, Harry. Make it a double."

Glenn isn't in this scene. It's just Sigourney and the guy who plays Kimberly's father. He hasn't been heard from yet. He's sitting at the far end of the table. His face might be familiar to people who watched daytime dramas in the '80's. His teeth still look the same.

"Yes, Daddy," says Sigourney, and she really sounds like she's talking to her daddy, "he was the one that told me I need to come clean with you and Mom."

"He said 'come clean'? He must be an old guy like me."

"His name is Harry Filmore. You'd like him, Daddy."

"Sounds like a good guy, Kimby-Nimby."

"You could really use a friend right now, couldn't you, Daddy?"

"Last night," he says, "she called me 'old man'. I had just suggested we should turn off the TV and get some peace and quiet for a change. So she called me 'old man' in mild disgust. I smiled, Kimmy, but five seconds later I felt a wave of anger and depression pass through me. At a time when I'm feeling so depressed already about getting older, it really punched me in the gut. I left the room and went upstairs. She knew I was mad. I was hurt and angry,

I felt I had to say something to her or else it would eat at me for hours. But I gradually started thinking about what caused your mom to say something so mean, and how she's going through so much physical and emotional trauma with her illness. And I realized I feel sorry for her right now, and now was not the time for me to be so hypersensitive and give her more grief. So I cooled down and my anger passed. She came up to bed and I kissed her goodnight."

"I love you, Daddy," says Sigourney and the scene finishes up and Stan starts to read the opening of the next scene. He's drowned out by the sound of sobbing. The sound is coming from Glenn's direction. Glenn is hiding his face, sobbing into his script, like he can't stop himself. Sigourney leans over with aching pity and wraps him in the arms and body that America once paid seven dollars at newsstands to see stapled in the center of Playpad Magazine.

NINETEEN

He told her several times that if she hears him talking to himself or yelling at thin air not to worry. It just means he's practicing his lines.

She assured him that nothing could shake her opinion of whether he is crazy or not.

He kind of seems to enjoy practicing his lines while he is doing things like warming up food or sitting in the bathroom. Today he is practicing a scene that the shooting schedule says will go forward on Day 2 of the shoot. He's got something warming up and the loud humming sound of the microwave could be imagined to be a noisy restaurant-bar where a Beverly Hills lawyer and his beautiful client are trying to talk.

"Let me finish, Andrea!" he says. He has to repeat it once or twice to get the right inflection. He says it to Vicky's wall calendar above the kitchen table. The calendar is Succulents From Around the World. "I am not shouting at you!" he says. "I'm just trying to be heard over this uproar. No, I am not on their side, I'm on your side. But you have to carry out your sentence, which by the way is a very fair sentence. Well I can't help it if Children's Hospital has rules that—. Andrea, you're not there to take over the hospital, you're there to do your volunteer hours and—. No, I'm sorry, if they tell you to file red files where the blue files go and blue files where the red files go, you just do it. Have you got that? Um, who is that big guy coming over from the bar? Who? You didn't tell me your boyfriend would be here. What do you mean he probably thinks I'm shouting at you? Miss, can we have our check please!"

The phone rings but Glenn starts doing the whole scene over again. He tones it down a little bit this time. He doesn't get very far before Vicky comes into the kitchen.

"That was Sierra on the phone."

"Oh? Do they want me at the studio or something?"

"No, Honey. It was for me."

"Oh. Uh—"

Vicky walks out of the kitchen. By the time he remembers his bowl of chili it will need another forty seconds in the microwave and he will eat it standing up and watching his wife look at things from her closet that she hasn't worn for a while and are still in the plastic from the dry cleaners that went out of business about six months before she retired.

Pasadena isn't anywhere in the script. But it has the best-looking courthouse so that's where they're doing a promotional photoshoot of the cast. It doesn't look like a courthouse, it was a fancy hotel a hundred years ago and eventually got converted into the Ninth Circuit Court of Appeals but it will look good on social media and Hollywood tabloids and maybe even big movie posters, when the time comes. They hired a famous photographer and he hired several assistants and there's a video person, too, in case they want to capture the process. And then there's Vicky.

Vicky is getting as much as she can on her phone. She's getting some pretty good stuff. And when there's a break she shows some of it to Sigourney and they giggle and Vicky sends her a few short clips in case she wants to enjoy them later or show them to Mr. Trombo. When you're Sigourney Trombo's reader or script assistant or all-around assistant or whatever words the actress used when she begged Stan to hire Vicky full-time, your official duties are not precisely set out.

When he's not being professionally posed looking thoughtful with his dark suit and legal pad and pen leaning against a palm tree on the main courthouse walkway, Glenn is mostly watching Vicky. He's watching her in a way that will probably be good practice for doing Harry Filmore in the scenes where Harry tries to understand his clients' behavior but can't. Vicky hasn't looked at him in half an hour. She is a one-woman cheering section for Sigourney, who is wearing a low-cut top and a short skirt and makes posing for a sexy photoshoot look as easy and natural as pouring a glass of skim milk. Rachel who plays Andrea and Porsha who plays Danielle have no problems looking sexy, either. The guy who plays Andrea's boyfriend has done some professional modeling. During the guy's session Glenn makes himself stand up straighter and hold his shoulders out. He is trying to stay in the shade, the sun is starting to get above the hills and trees of Pasadena. Pamela, who plays Harry's wife, loves the camera and the camera loves her. That's what the photographer tells her while he is shooting. He is friendly, he's giving lots of compliments and encouragement to all the actors when they're being shot. He also raves a lot about the light and the shadows and the colors and the softness of everything. He's a little impatient and nasty with his two assistants, the lighting person, the wardrobe lady, the makeup artist and the stylist, who all look stressed. The whole thing lasts a while. Most of the cast changes outfits once or twice. Glenn just has to take off his suit jacket and loosen his tie and stand with his arms crossed. The photographer gets a kick out of it.

After her last session, which is in a bathrobe for some reason, Sigourney runs over to Vicky and grabs her by one arm. She says she just got a text from Arthur. "He's flying in next week," she says. "He needs the endorsement of something called the Hoover Institution. Isn't that great? He can meet you. And Glenn."

"Oh, my," Vicky says.

It's a Saturday. Still early. Sigourney and her bodyguards take Vicky and Glenn to brunch after the photoshoot. Glenn doesn't offer to pay.

Every couple minutes she asks Glenn to fix the hose. She means get the kink out because there's only a little trickle coming out of the nozzle and her geraniums and roses need more than a trickle. Since this is one of the few things that Glenn can fix around the house, he doesn't complain about marking the page in his Stephen King novel every couple minutes and getting up from his lawn chair and getting the kink out and sitting down again, even though Vicky's backyard watering takes about forty-five minutes. They don't have to have that conversation about the fact that the hose was labeled "Kink-Free" when they bought it and it was a $44.99 hose and it started kinking when they uncoiled it the first time and it hasn't stopped kinking since and getting the kink out in one place means it will immediately show up in another. They had that conversation months ago, when the warranty on the hose was still good.

When Vicky finishes she gets to sit by Glenn and eat an orange that she just picked and look at her phone. She lets Claudia put her front paws on her thigh and get petted a little bit. "That's enough," she says and makes the shaggy mutt lie down. She tells her what a good girl she is. She looks at her fingers and flicks off the dog hairs.

Vicky smiles. She looks at the pair of Wrentits eating birdseed on the ground near the patio and the pair of Spotted Towhees by the bushes and the finches and sparrows and Claudia who has no interest in birds but likes to chase a squirrel now and then.

"I wonder why that woodpecker is eating my birdseed," she says.

Glenn looks over at the bird feeder where a black and white and gray woodpecker with a red crown is perched and pecking seeds. Glenn sits very still. "Probably on a low worm diet," he says.

He looks at Vicky out of the corner of his eye. She is eyeing him back, with doubt. The only ones smiling are Claudia and the floating skull on the cover of Glenn's book.

It's very Noir.

Marilyn the 1st AD is talking to them about the scene. They all know the backstory. Kimberly's dad just died suddenly so Harry, whether he likes it or not, becomes a convenient father figure at such a vulnerable time for Kimberly. "You both look very nice," Marilyn says. "And this is just a rehearsal." She looks at her phone. "You've got time for coffee. I'll be back."

Glenn looks around the room like he could use a cigarette. Glenn has never had a cigarette in his life and can't stand to be in a place where cigarettes are allowed. "Sigourney, who is that guy watching us?"

"Oh, that's Bruce my new manager."

"What happened to your old manager?"

"He still is. Bruce is just an extra manager for this project."

"Why do you think you need an extra manager?"

"Arthur thought it would be a good idea. He's very involved in my career."

"Bruce doesn't look like the artistic type."

"Arthur hired him from one of the best talent agencies. It's called Blackwater."

"Okay." Glenn swallows.

"Arthur had him show me how to play a love scene without touching."

"Arthur knows about this scene?"

"I asked him to rehearse it with me. It was fun."

"Arthur is here in L.A.?"

She shakes her head. "Phoenix. We did it by video chat. I think Arthur would be a great actor if he had the time."

"Sigourney, I'm a little unsure about the, um, blocking of this scene. Let's talk to Stan. Let's see if we can't modify a couple things? Hmmmh? Or even delete. Where did Vicky go?"

"She wanted to video a production meeting, and they're having one now, I think."

"Sierra," Glenn says across the practice set that if you look sideways and imagine hard enough could be the office of some big Beverly Hills lawyer but would make a better bus station. The 2nd AD looks up from her annotated shooting schedule. "How many black belts," he says loud enough for Bruce to hear, "do you have in martial arts. I can't keep track."

162

The low clouds are starting to roll in, they don't care where Brentwood turns into Bellaire, or where Bellaire ends and Beverly Hills begins. They roll over gated and ungated communities without prejudice. Glenn takes off his sunglasses and only has to squint a little.

He wanted to park on the street but Vicky wouldn't let him. While he stands by the wide front steps and gets scanned with a hand-held metal detector and has his picture taken he watches his car going around the side of the house faster than he drove it on the 405 to get here.

It's Vicky's turn to get scanned but someone says "Cool it, Benson. They're clean." Morales, the head bodyguard who works for Mrs. Trombo and almost threw Vicky out of the Hong Kong Café a few weeks ago is walking toward her with his hands up. "You look very sharp, Mr. and Mrs. Stover. Everyone is relaxing around the pool. I know a shortcut." He leads them inside and down some hallways and through a den and out a patio door. The TV in the den is on and tuned to that news channel that likes to make up its own news. When all the other networks are covering President Brown holding a press conference about the need to pass his environmental plan before the end of his second term or covering the latest mass shooting, it's the station that will be doing an in-depth story on the time that Senator Merrill marched in a May Day parade when she was 17. Vicky and Glenn follow the large guy past the tennis courts and over to Mrs. Trombo.

Sigourney is helping the caterers with the hors d'oeuvres. Everything is Basque cuisine. Once when they were in Europe she had Basque food and thought it was the best thing ever. She's carrying a platter of anchovy tapas. The head caterer is trying to talk Sigourney into joining her guests and relaxing but she won't and shakes her head but then she sees the Stovers and runs to meet them with the tray in her arms like someone bringing a small trampoline to catch somebody who wants to jump from a burning building. "I wanted to wait for you in the driveway but Arthur doesn't like me doing things that look needy."

Glenn takes the tray while they do the hugs. Glenn doesn't eat anchovies. Sigourney is excited about Vicky's dress. She took her shopping and helped her pick it out. She's excited about how dolled up Vicky is. They're giggling even though Vicky can hardly smile because she has too much makeup. Glenn knew better than to say anything. He had to buy a new suit if he wanted his wife to talk to him. He's approaching the whole evening like Spencer Tracy in Father of the Bride.

"Let's go meet Arthur." Sigourney pulls Vicky by the hand. They go past the bar and the jazz trio. They go around the pool. At the foot of the diving board Mr. Trombo is sipping a Scotch and talking to a lady who is chilly but holding a jacket. Trombo's eyes are on his wife coming his way. He grins. It's the same grin as when he talks about outsourcing the National Park Service. His arm is extended, the one without the Scotch. It must be very clear to the guy that his luscious wife expects to be squeezed. And to give him one of her sloppy kisses. Before introducing her special friends.

"Guess who, Arthur?" Her shoulders work up and down like pistons until Trombo clamps her by the waist. "Who haven't I stopped talking about for the last five weeks?" she says with a lot of breath an inch away from his nose. It's a pretty good nose.

"She ain't kidding." The voice of Trombo. It's a deep voice on television but without a microphone or cameras it rumbles out like it's brought up in buckets from a dark vein of anthracite. "She ain't stopped raving about Vicky and Glenn, Vicky and Glenn," says the rich tycoon. "Since she started the damn picture." He stares at Vicky. He smooths his hair back. He tells her that his little Kitten here told him her friend was stunning and boy did she nail it. His little Kitten is giggling and he gives her an extra squeeze which seems to push more giggles out. Possibly more than what's necessarily healthy.

"Say, Glenn," says Trombo, "what a pleasure to meet someone where we have such a lot in common."

Glenn's eyes widen and it's the face of a guy who was just picked out of a lineup.

"This is so great," Sigourney says while the husbands shake hands. She squeezes Vicky and they gush and giggle like they just met up at the prom and their dates are parking the cars.

Trombo orders them drinks. The two couples chat around a patio table with an umbrella. The low clouds are breaking up as fast as they roll in and the whole sky is on a dimmer switch that is slowly revolving clockwise and controls orange footlights in the west. The Stovers talk about how beautiful the mansion is and how gorgeous the yard is and how great the pool is and the Trombos talk about how wonderful and special the Stovers are and how glad they are that they could join them tonight for this little shindy. This little wingding. This little clambake, this little fiesta, this little mixer, this little pajama party, this little hootenanny. Glenn is getting a kick out of Trombo's witty style. And the way he finishes his drinks and yells "*Garcon*".

Trombo calls a young guy over and you would say that the young guy speaks the same body language as his father. Punctuated by the same red widow's peak except that the young guy goes to a salon and gets his whole head trimmed with something that's plugged in to a wall socket and you would need a ruler with millimeters to measure the hair that isn't on the floor of the salon. The effect can be stark. Depending on what the guy's forehead is doing. Right now his forehead is pushing his eyebrows out with a penetrating glare. "Adam. Meet our friends Glenn and Vicky Stover."

This is an introduction that didn't need to be made. Adam Trombo knows who the Stovers are. Adam

Trombo doesn't even try to pretend that he doesn't know who the Stovers are just as well as his dad knows who the Stovers are. And everybody knows Adam Trombo. And the job he's done as Trombo Campaign Manager for California. Trombo is telling them now what a job his son has done as Trombo Campaign Manager for California. Vicky is nodding. Vicky's eyes are on those sharp widow's peaks both aimed at the economic and geopolitical world.

Glenn's eyes are on Vicky. His walking political barometer.

Adam asks how the picture is going. Then he asks when it will be over. He says he has campaign speeches for Sigourney to give to a handful of women's groups over the next two weeks. He says his assistant can help her pick out something a little less, um, exposed than the way she usually dresses. He looks at her neckline, then at her legs. He says they've missed her on the campaign trail. Now he's looking at Vicky. Sigourney's staring at her drink like it might make a good projectile.

"It's true, Kitten," says Trombo. He wipes both nostrils with the back of his hand and sniffs. "Everybody out there in America is asking where's Sigourney, where's your stunning wife. I gotta shrug my shoulders and crack a joke."

"They are not," says Sigourney. "Anyway we only just started our shooting schedule, we still have all the big scenes, don't we, Glenn?"

"I'll betcha Kitten that that director'll give you a few days off if you ask him."

"He can't, Arthur, he's got everything all planned out, you should see how organized everything is. They're very serious business people, just like you."

"Dad." Adam's head and its red stubble start pushing up on the spokes of the umbrella. They're the sharp kind. Glenn looks up and scoots his chair closer to Vicky. "Remember what you always taught us? You can't put a price on loyalty? Especially family? I don't see how a member of our family can, can—"

"I have loyalty. Arthur when have I ever—"

"—put their personal ambition ahead of the family."

"—not been loyal? I just don't like speaking in public. I'm terrified of it."

"I don't think you're terrified, Miss Big Famous Hollywood Starlet, I think you're brainwashed. Somebody's been a bad influence on you." Trombo junior turns his blue eyes on the Stovers and the Stovers look like they're taking a course in movie slaps from one of the Three Stooges.

"That's not nice, Adam." Sigourney pushes herself away from the table and stands up. "You should know better, you're older than me." She scoops up her guests, one Stover in each arm, and leaves the table.

"Now, Kitten—" The jazz trio is playing Trombo's favorite song, My Foolish Heart. The piano is smooth as ice.

Two widow's peaks the color of Tandoori point at each other. Two Trombos are left alone to size each other up. A picture that might make even an authority on the fighting roosters of rural Pennsylvania scratch his head.

Dinner is nice. Nobody's talking politics. There isn't assigned seating around the table like in Jane Austen's time, people just sit wherever their impulses tell them to sit. Or they ignore their impulses and contend with all the social ramifications.

The guy who is West Coast Director of the Trombo Enterprise Group is here with his wife. The guy who raised twenty million dollars for various pro-Trombo PAC's is here with his new girlfriend. The guy who is not a judge or even a lawyer and who's always on television advertising his self-cleaning toilet and whom Trombo says he'll appoint to the Supreme Court because he wants lay people to be represented on the Supreme Court is here with his wife who has a thirty-minute podcast called "The God and Truth Hour". The Congresswoman who says the Governor of California should be impeached for letting middle school kids read books that were written by foreigners and votes against every liberal or moderate bill including her party's own budget package is here with her husband. Her husband is here with their Papillon toy spaniel. From his lap Dixie can just see over the edge of the table. She already had a little plate of catering scraps that was arranged prettier than most restaurant meals but her little nose doesn't stop twitching in all foodward directions. Mega-donor Dante Dove, that hawkish pop singer who is separated from his wife the wristwatch heiress is here with his guitar. A string broke when he sat in with the jazz trio on "You'd Be So Nice To Come Home To" and he's taking it out on the veal. Dr. Sheldon Smith whom Glenn shakes hands with without mentioning that he heard the knowledgeable orthodontist talk about deep state theories last spring at an Independents for Trombo meeting is here with his wife. Mrs. Smith doesn't like the okra dish and spoons most of it over onto her husband's plate.

They eat well or they force themselves to eat. They try everything or they put up a hand to some of the servers when they find out what that mysterious-looking thing is on the platter. They finish their ice water for the second time and look around with their tongue dangling or they eat steadily while their ice cubes melt under the bright offset lighting. They frown as though even a fancy dinner party with the next President doesn't eclipse the lousiness of life or they smile as though life is nothing but one big fancy party. They use their napkin like they're creating an original oil on linen for the Museum of Contemporary Art or they use it like it's going straight in the trash. They ask questions or they let the other person do the asking. They talk or they listen. They seek eye contact or they fear eye contact. They talk and chew or they chew first, talk later. They occasionally let their eyes wander to the flowers and the Renoir and the Picasso and the Aboriginal figurines and all the other posh furnishings or they never look beyond the other faces and bodies and hairdos and plates of food. They watch the servers like watching a movie about The Depression or they simply couldn't care less if catering workers are tall or thin or pale or old. They get up whenever they need to use the bathroom or they sit like there's one of those pranksters around who still thinks glue on the chair seat is funny. They sway or nod occasionally to the music or they move to some other unidentified music that isn't playing, possibly Twinkle Twinkle or The Candyman Can. They let go and interact and connect and use the facial expressions they've been using all their life or they keep their personality encrypted like you need a password to get in. They blink and laugh and roll their eyes and dislodge food with their tongue and shift their weight and sniff repeatedly and groan at dessert. Or they don't.

Nobody's talking politics. Except Trombo offers Glenn a political appointment like Ambassador to Guam, or an appointment to be on one of his White House Advisory Committees, when he gets elected. Glenn can choose which one. Sigourney gets excited for Glenn. Trombo thinks the Advisory Committee on Bias in Public Radio and Television would be a good one. "Whadya think, Glenn? Are ya up for it?"

The whole table is interested in the idea. Somebody suggests the Advisory Committee on Unnecessary Government Travel.

"Bingo," says Trombo. "Those guys get the best expense accounts. Huh, Glenn?" Trombo is snickering. He could elbow Glenn in the ribs except they're three people apart.

Glenn is flushed, he's smiling. Everybody's looking. Trombo's still snickering. Trombo knows how to direct a snicker. He can direct it to a general audience as well as to individual members of that audience. Both the mouth and the eyes are involved, so you could tell it's a bona fide snicker with a sound-only version or a picture-only version. But the sound plus picture version is indisputable.

Glenn starts chuckling. It's a chuckle but it's not Glenn's normal chuckle, it's as close to a snicker as Glenn normally gets. Snickering is something Glenn might do in an acting role or joking around with Vicky or the kids but not in real life. Glenn grins at Trombo. Vicky looks at Glenn's grin like there might be pain involved.

Dr. Smith is reminded of a dentist joke he picked up recently at a conference. "Guy's in the dentist chair. Dentist looks in the guy's mouth and starts shaking his head and clicking his tongue. 'My oh my. You have an awfully big cavity there, Mr. Lewis.' 'Gosh, how big is it, Doc?' 'It's so big,' says the dentist, 'Trombo wants to build his next petrochemical plant there!'"

When you're having dinner with the Trombos, and the joke is about something big and somebody wants to know how big, and Trombo himself is the punchline, you've got very little choice. You've got to produce laughter just as hysterical and just as long and just as drawn out as everybody else. Nobody wants to get on Trombo's bad side by being the wet blanket at a love fest in his honor.

When everyone feels it's safe to stop laughing, the self-cleaning toilet guy starts swaying to the soft background music and conducting it in the air. It's a piano sonata. "Ah, Chopin," he says. "Perfect dinner companion." Like he really knows classical music.

Glenn is trying his fish and vegetable stew: "I think that's Schubert, actually. Piano Sonata in B Flat Major."

Vicky swallows a bite of spicy sausage with sauce from sheep's cheese. It will be at least a minute before she would be able to say the words sheep's cheese. The toilet guy is staring at Glenn and his mouth is the shape of his Elongated Upflush model. Trombo looks at Sigourney. The way he cuts his grilled leg of lamb it could be Medicare being hacked from the budget.

"I ordered this CD from Zonian, Arthur. I just know it's called Beloved Love Songs from the Classics. It sounded like the kind of music that Glenn likes."

Trombo smiles around the table. Vicky shivers. There are lipstick lips on Vicky's wine glass but except for one or two sips it's still full of wine.

Adam Trombo spends most of the dinner talking in a low voice to his wife or calling one of the Secret Service guys over to have a word. He doesn't touch any of the Basque dishes, he just takes some pickles, some plain rice, and garlic butter.

After dinner they all move back out to the pool area and have coffee and after-dinner drinks. Vicky and Glenn try to sit by one of the propane heaters. One of the women sitting nearby starts asking Glenn how he got into acting, what other things he's been in and what it's like being in a Hollywood picture and going to premiers. Glenn downplays the glamor and tries not to look at Vicky while he's talking. Pretty soon Sigourney comes and pulls them both out of their chairs. She leads them inside to her bedroom to show them her photo albums and her clothes and her cosmetics and her momentos from being a Playpad Kitten. Glenn falls asleep in an armchair while the girls are giggling and looking at the old issues of Playpad where Sigourney was one of the featured Kittens.

"Pussycat." Trombo stands in the doorway. "What's goin on? Hmmmh? Your guests are wondering where the hell you are."

"I had to show Vicky my stuff, Arthur. I don't really feel comfortable with those people."

"Those people are—" He looks down at her like she's been a bad, bad girl but she might get off with a warning this time. "I need you there, Kitten. You're my fabulous hostess."

"I know." She turns a color that she never turned when she was posing for the magazine. "We're coming, Arthur. As soon as Glenn wakes up."

"Maybe Vicky here will give him a nice big wet one," he says, "right on the chops. That oughta wake him pronto."

"Arthur," she says. "Talk nice."

Glenn wakes himself up a few minutes later with a single explosive snore. Sigourney takes the Stovers back outside and Trombo makes a big fuss over her and has her sit on his lap until his leg falls asleep and he kicks her off. Everyone is getting friendly and acquainted and talking about their kids or their houses or their trips and there are several conversations going on around the pool but everyone has at least one ear tuned to Trombo and anything he might happen to say.

When Dante Dove gets up to go inside to use the bathroom Vicky overhears Trombo in a low voice trying to be funny and make some suggestive remark about the singer's race behind his back to one of the ladies. Vicky looks to see if Glenn heard but Glenn is munching pita chips and checking his phone to see if there's anything new from the studio. Sigourney is quiet, sitting back in her patio chair smiling, and when she feels Vicky's hand on hers she turns to her friend with a brave face and a tiny shrug.

"Arthur, why don't you show the Stovers how well you play the piano. And Dante could sing while you play. When he gets back from the bathroom. Wouldn't that be nice?"

"I ain't played in too long, Pussycat. You play."

"I don't know how, Arthur."

"So you bang the keys around a little bit. Nobody's gonna say anything. It's your party."

"That's silly, Arthur."

"You know it's funny. I had a Mrs. Stover for a piano teacher when I was a kid. I remember she lived over by that old Ormsby Mansion where those snooty art people lived. I showed you, remember, when I took you back to the old burg after we got hitched?"

"I just remember it was the cutest little town, like a tiny little village."

"Yeah. And this old lady Stover had a grandson that used to come out for the summers and stay with her. And he was a scrawny little kid and I remember I beat him up the first time I saw him and then we became best friends." On Trombo's face flickers a faraway look that nobody at the party had ever seen before. "Any kind of trouble we could get into, anywhere in town, that was for us. Not that you could get into anything too terrible awful in Ebensburg. Geez, those were the days."

Glenn is sitting up straight. He is looking strange under the propane flame. "What town did you—"

"Ebensburg. Ebensburg, Pennsylvania. Why, every time we got caught in some kind of monkey business, old lady Stover—"

"—was my Grandma."

"What's that you say, Glenn?"

"Artie!"

"Spanky?"

Sitting up in her lawn chair Vicky stiffens. She stares a stare of disbelief into the depths of the sparkling pool. She mouths the name Spanky.

The TV in the den is talking about Trombo's pledge to make welfare fraud in the District of Columbia carry a mandatory life sentence. The anchor is interviewing the Congressman from Colorado who recently did a post on social media that anyone who applies for welfare should be required to wear a giant W on their forehead. If you click on the social media post it will take you to a link for donating to his reelection campaign. He's raised 1.8 million in the last seven days.

TWENTY

He never expected to have to see the inside of Parker Center again but he's sounding kind of sentimental and smug as he leads some crew members to the old lock-up area where they're shooting this morning and he's pointing out all the old familiar places to Vicky and to the crew members whose arms are full of vast quantities of equipment worth more than any of their salaries.

"That's where protesters broke in, or tried to break in, after Rodney King," he says. "That was very convenient. Officers didn't need to call for backup or transport, they just cuffed the subjects and walked them sixty feet back to booking." Vicky looks like she would have been rooting for the protesters. Possibly leading them.

"Glenn, where's the nearest ladies room?"

"I think there's one somewhere in the building."

He points out a door down one of the hallways. "That was the conference room that Homicide Detectives used to use. I think I was the last Deputy D.A. to have a meeting there. That was the Brinkerhoff case, the guy who shot his tennis partner for calling a lob in instead of long. Nobody ever knew who actually won the point, and the match was called on account of spurting blood. We were picking the jury the day they started shutting this place down and moving everything over to Main Street. Boy I never thought this place would be a gold mine for Hollywood production companies. I wish I'd thought of it."

Vicky rolls her eyes for a second but then she sees a restroom and runs.

Sigourney arrives on set looking like they started paying her by the ounce of lip gloss, and hobbling.

"Why are you limping, Sigs?" Vicky helps her to a stool. Vicky's only seven inches shorter. The stool is the kind that's bolted down. Just like the ones on the other side of the bulletproof glass. Both sides could use some new upholstery. Between attorneys and criminals there's no difference when it comes to sitting in uncomfortable places and wearing out the material faster than anyone intended.

The actress says she woke up with a sprained ankle. It wasn't sprained when she went to bed. But it hurt so much when she was dreaming that she was late for her flight to somewhere and was limping up the hill. This airport had a hill. Then she woke up and her foot was in a funny position and she cried and couldn't walk to the bathroom. "What am I trying to prove, Vick? I mean it, Vicky, how stupid am I?" She squints up. The lighting guy has things turned on full blast and is fiddling with angles. "Kimberly is like twenty something and I'm twice, no, more than twice! There's no way I can pretend to be twenty something anymore. Look at my neck. It's got circles. Arthur's right, who am I kidding? I don't belong in movies. I'm an embarrassment to the family, his whole family hates me. I don't belong in the White House. I don't know how to act like a White House lady."

Vicky takes a big breath and blows it out slowly. "Honey, you haven't won the election yet, you might not have to worry about all that stuff if he—" She stops because Sigourney's mouth opens like a bowl of shredded dreams. Vicky swallows. "You are a queen," she says, like a mom to a scared little girl on her first day of charm school. She will be the most stunning First Lady ever. America will love her. America already loves her. She's an amazing actor, everybody on the production loves her and raves about her performances. "Glenn thinks you're better than Hepburn."

Vicky talks to her for a while about what really matters when you come right down to the essence of your identity, your self-esteem. If she feels young inside she will look young on the outside. It will automatically be conveyed to the audience. She sort of coaches her in simplified acting method. Sigourney just listens quietly. Glenn nods occasionally and writes notes on his script like he's getting an introduction to Stanislavski. Afterwards while Sigourney goes to fix her face with the makeup lady and call her husband and tell him how happy she is and how much she loves the Stovers, Glenn puts his arm around Vicky. "Hey, Stella Adler. Where'd you get all that stuff, I didn't know you knew all about acting. The motivation? The actor's instrument?"

"I'm a renowned thespian, didn't you know?"

Sigourney comes back cheerful and upbeat and gazing at her phone. She says Arthur took her call right away. She says he's in Orlando giving a speech to the American Association of Correctional Corporations about the need to double the number of prison facilities and increase the maximum sentences of all federal crimes other than white collar. She reads it to Vicky and Glenn from a news article on her phone that Arthur sent her.

Glenn wants to know if she told him Spanky says hi. "I didn't, Glenn. I'm such a dunce. I'll call him back."

"No, no, no, I'm just kidding." He stares at his scene partner for a couple seconds. Like she's a mystery that hasn't been solved and probably is better off left that way.

Stan Elway the Director and Marilyn the 1st AD and Glenn and Sigourney have a conference about the scene. Stan thinks it will be great. When it's almost time to go do blocking Glenn starts to get ready to stand up. He changes his mind. "Do the phones still actually work?" he says. "That glass is soundproof, too."

Stan says "Oh" and says Glenn is the first person who thought about that. He looks more pleased than irritated. "But you don't really need the phones to work, you both know your lines."

"But we won't know exactly when to jump in. It'll throw off our reactions." Glenn looks from Stan to Sigourney and Stan looks from Glenn to Marilyn. Marilyn sends Ramin the sound guy to check the phones. They've been disconnected, who knows how long ago. It takes about five minutes for the crew to come up with a technical solution and about half an hour to rig it up and test it and make it foolproof. They tape a cell phone on each side of the glass, out of frame from the camera, and connect a call between the two and put them on speaker. They test Glenn's voice on the contrivance. He can hear and be heard. He smiles.

Sigourney takes her place on the stool on the other side of the glass. She's wearing street clothes, Kimberly has only been in custody overnight on a probation violation and didn't have to wear a blue jumpsuit. Sigourney was disappointed when she found out. "I really wanted to wear jail clothes and look like a criminal. It would have been so much fun."

The first shot is going to be a medium shot over Glenn's shoulder looking at Sigourney through the glass. To be in frame the camera operator has Glenn lean a little to the left. A little more. A little more. Now a little to the right. Thumbs up. Now lean forward a little.

"Try not to move too much," the guy says. His glasses are the kind with a little yellow tint so you can't tell what he's really thinking. "But without impeding your acting." The makeup lady touches up the powder on Glenn's face. He thanks her. One young guy keeps asking everyone if they want more water or a banana. The bananas are popular.

There's prolific discussion among all levels of crew members who are setting up the shot. It's true democracy, there has to be a consensus. Only the actors are left out of the conversation. Sigourney seems to know exactly where they are and what is going on but Glenn sits veiled in ignorance. Marilyn says "Roll sound" and Ramin says "Sound rolling" and Glenn looks around like any second now somebody is going to clue him in. Nobody does.

"Roll camera."

"Camera rolling."

Glenn peers through the glass at Sigourney who looks relaxed and then closes her eyes to get into character.

"Is this a take or just a—" Glenn says it over his shoulder but not at anyone in particular because there's no one paying any attention to him at the moment, until they call "Action" he's just a human prop. The closest person is the Assistant Gaffer, who finishes switching some wires and gives him a sweet smile equal to 9700 lumens. She tells him it's a take. Glenn sits up and flexes his shoulders a few times. He moistens his lips. He stares through the glass like he's the one that got caught holding the bag.

They have Shakira the scene board person mark the scene and everyone puts themselves on mute and finally Stan says "Action".

The probation violation is for opening all the cages at the Animal Shelter and letting all the animals out through the back door because she felt sorry for them and couldn't stand seeing them locked up anymore, it's been gnawing at Kimberly for weeks and she finally just snapped and now she's in big trouble and she's really sorry and remorseful because she didn't think about the consequences like the poor animals could get run over on the highway after she let them escape which would be worse than being locked up at the Animal Shelter. It's funny how Kimberly's dialogue sounds suspiciously like Sigourney's normal way of talking.

"I couldn't help it, Harry, they were looking at me with their little faces through those wires and I couldn't take it anymore. Now they're all back safe and sound, poor little things, but I bet they're sadder than ever. They tasted freedom and now they're back in jail. Like me. Poor little Francisco, with his little black nose and his little paws stuck through the wires looking at me. I'm gonna adopt him, Harry." Sigourney bursts into sobs, she's terrific, the whole crew is watching and blinking. In a couple days they'll be shooting the little scene at the Animal Shelter, she's been bouncing and babbling about it constantly.

"You tied my hands Kimberly, I got nothin. You're going to have to throw yourself on the Court's mercy, this little stunt of yours is a first, in the history of community service. The Judge gave you every break, you saw how serious she was about rehabilitation. Now you've made a mockery of her and her courtroom." Glenn looks full of pain and frustration but partly because he just pinched his little finger in the twisty steel cord that anchors the heavy black phone that attorneys use to talk to their bad clients.

After the medium shot they readjust. This time it's a close up of Sigourney so Glenn's head and shoulder aren't in it and it's just both their voices and Sigourney's face through the glass. Vicky keeps giving Sigourney a thumbs up with her eyes wide and sincere. Stan thinks it's looking great. He and Claire the cinematographer watch most of the takes on the monitor attached to the camera. And sometimes they go watch it on a separate monitor. Directors and cinematographers love certain colors, shadows, light effects and camera angles. They see everything through the camera lens. Claire is very serious and quiet and doesn't make eye contact with Glenn, she lets the camera do that. She and Glenn were introduced once but that's about it.

Once in a while they have to call time out to change discs or batteries, or fiddle with Glenn's microphone which is taped to his undershirt under his dress shirt and looped to the transmitter in his right front pants pocket. Glenn is constantly looking down where the microphone is hidden and fidgeting like he's afraid he just pulled it loose. They move the camera around to Sigourney's side to do the shots of Glenn over her shoulder and through the glass. First the medium shot. Each time they do two or three takes. Each time from the top. By the time they do his close up, Glenn is yawning.

"I messed up a couple of times," he says after the second take. He did, too.

Stan shakes his head. "You were great."

Glenn looks at Vicky like he's ready for a nap and asks her for some cashews. She gives him a pretty good handful from a bag in her backpack that she stashed outside of camera range. Then he needs water. He smiles and gets Vicky to check his teeth for cashew flecks. They do two more takes including the last one that Stan and Claire think about for a second while everybody holds their breath and then Stan says "one more just for safety".

Stan decides he wants a long shot from way behind Glenn that shows his whole body and Sigourney's upper body and the stools and the glass and the Nixon-era linoleum and a lot of the general visiting area. So they move the camera equipment back to the other side which takes twenty minutes. They do a couple takes of the whole scene from that angle and they both give probably their best performances of the day and you can hardly see their faces. Then Stan says "Moving on" and Marilyn says "Moving on" and everyone looks like they look when they get money back from the Franchise Tax Board.

The rest of the day they just have lunch and shoot little easy shots that don't need dialogue, like a moving close up of Sigourney's feet and fancy shoes and the guard's feet and black oxfords when they're walking to the visiting area or Glenn's hands wiping off the phone receiver with an alcohol pad before he puts it to his ear. And a shot of Sigourney just crying tragically when Kimberly comes through the lock-up door and sees Harry sitting there.

They wrap early and nobody needs to stand on ceremony or be particularly polite about saying goodbyes all around because they'll all be back together in the morning for another day's shoot in some location which Glenn usually tells Vicky he hopes will be someplace less than a forty-five minute drive from home, and he hopes will have decent bathrooms. The Stovers walk Sigourney to the Parker Center parking lot that isn't used anymore unless you're with the Los Angeles Department of Building and Safety or the demolition engineering firm they hired to do a report, or unless you're an even bet to be the next First Lady. They want to see her new Bentley which she just leased in Beverly Hills because she likes the way you can walk down Wilshire Boulevard past the huge windows where you can look right into the glitzy showrooms and see the big imported sedans that nobody knows how they got them in there. The three friends get in and sit while her security and Secret Service sit in their cars parked on both sides and Glenn and Sigourney have time to run their lines for the courtroom scene related to today's scene that they'll be shooting on Friday. First Sigourney shows Vicky how the steering wheel has little individually-adjustable air conditioning vents to keep her fingers cool and dry. "Isn't that ingenious?" she says.

Vicky reads the Judge's lines. "Ms. Van Winkle." She tries to sound like the actress who plays the Judge. She and Sigourney are leaning their heads together in the front seats that Sigourney adjusted for maximum comfort with six different electronic controls. They're sharing Sigourney's script. As her personal script consultant Vicky stuck lots of post-its in it. "Is it your profound wish to spend the next three years in State Prison? Because that's how it looks to me."

"We pled to the mid-term, Your Honor." Glenn is in the back seat with his script. He has it mostly memorized but he's referring to it out of sheer nonchalance.

"Maybe Ms. Van Winkle wants to open all the cages at the prison and let all the convicts run free." Vicky sees the Judge getting a little sardonic and a little exasperated here.

"I'm sorry, Your Honor. I was so dumb. Dumb, dumb, dumb. I didn't think, I just. I just couldn't bear the cruelty of those poor little doggies and kitties and bunnies and birdies being locked up like that and being so afraid. It was breaking my heart. If you had seen them, Your Honor, you would have—" Sigourney lets herself get a little choked up here and Vicky gives her a little nod of encouragement.

"Well, Ms. Van Winkle," Vicky says, "Ordinarily, I take violations of probation very seriously. In this case, however, I think in a strange contorted kind of way we have a situation of someone whose heart is in the right place and had a momentary lapse of judgment. I also think we have someone who is extraordinarily remorseful for what she has done. The whole point of the sentence was to learn to think about others, albeit animals, more than yourself. And I think that's exactly what you're learning. If I give you another chance, do you think you can complete your community service without absolutely wreaking havoc upon the world?"

Sigourney doesn't have a line here, she's just supposed to nod her head vigorously and bawl.

"Very well, in that case I find you in violation of probation but probation is reinstated on the same terms and conditions with credit for one day served. That'll be the order. This is a gimme, Mr. Filmore. Any more shenanigans from your clients and I will send them up the river."

"I am eternally grateful, Your Honor."

"Gratitude I don't need, Mr. Filmore. Compliance is the thing that butters my bread."

Vicky turns, grins, and sticks her tongue out at her husband. They all sit back and tell each other how great they did with the reading, and Sigourney plays with the buttons that open and close the sun roof and asks them if they want to come to Pennsylvania with her and Arthur for election night. "It's like a big party," she says, "and Arthur gets to make a speech and he says he'll be President by ten o'clock Pittsburgh time." She giggles.

Glenn is staring through the sun roof. He blinks a few times. About a hundred pigeons are swooping and circling above the parking lot. Last night Vicky let him watch TCM, he caught the last forty minutes of The Birds and Ben Mankiewicz summing up about Tippi Hedren and how she got along with Hitchcock and which direction her career went after that picture. Glenn always gives Vicky a letdown look if they watch a movie on another channel and there's no TCM host summing up after the credits.

After The Birds Vicky told Glenn he better not have a nightmare and kick her in his sleep. He had a nightmare but he didn't kick her this time. He only screamed.

Vicky doesn't have to dream about birds, she has them in real life where she can bond with them like grandchildren. This morning was gray and drizzly so Vicky and her plants and her birds are all happy and are in the yard where they are all happiest, even when the sun starts to lunge through. Glenn is in his lawn chair with a Cornell Woolrich murder mystery and is also happy because he's not on the shooting schedule for today. But Glenn looks alarmingly less happy when the morning quiet is broken by certain words.

"You know what else we could move?" Seven small words.

And yet one of the leading questions that husbands generally never want to hear from their wives. Glenn also looks confused, even Cornell Woolrich might have a hard time figuring out a question that, at a particular place and time, lacks any antecedent whatsoever. The last thing Glenn and Vicky moved was two weeks ago and it was in the front yard and it involved digging.

Happily, it's only a concrete birdbath that Vicky wants to move this morning, not a china hutch or the living room set. So Glenn is still in a good mood when the birdbath is installed in its new spot and he offers out of sheer good will to go pick up lunch from the Ruby of Siam Restaurant, which they got a coupon for in yesterday's junk mail.

When he gets back with their takeout and puts it on the kitchen counter Glenn gives Vicky the funny dialogue he had with the people at the restaurant. First they asked him if he wants paper or plastic, he says. The cashier was a young girl around eighteen with narrow hands and fancy nail polish and glasses.

"Um, paper."

"Would you like extra soy sauce?" A young guy was standing there helping. "I already gave you hot sauce."

Glenn hands Vicky the little packets of extra soy sauce. She's taking all the cartons out of the bag and opening them to see how they look.

"How about some Thai crispy crepe for dessert? It's included."

"Okay." Glenn points to the bag of little exotic pastries. Vicky is sniffing all the open cartons, taking deep breaths and closing her eyes like it's decongestant.

"Do you want your receipt?"

Glenn always smiles at cashiers and says "Sure", and sometimes he says "Keeps me organized" so he doesn't come across as a jerk.

"They have a lot of questions for you." The older lady walking up behind the counter was probably the owner. She had perfect comedic timing. She grinned at Glenn.

"I wasn't prepared for that," he told the lady. There was something about the way they all looked at each other and laughed at that moment that made him feel so good, he tells Vicky. "It was cute," he says. "Makes me wanna go back there, often."

Vicky seems to think it was very cute, too, but not enough to make her wait any longer to fill her plate with Pad Thai noodles and cucumber salad and shrimp curry.

While they eat their lunch and wait for Vicky's daytime drama Love For Tomorrow, they watch the end of that daily entertainment show with the hosts that know everybody's names and faces in Hollywood to the point that they get to do the Red Carpet almost every year and can pretty much name their price. Their last guest today is that singer from Ecuador who won a Grammy last year in the Dance/Electronic category. They're sitting on stools with her in the middle and asking her about her acting debut in the big feature film that is being released this week. She hardly has any accent. She talks about her character in the movie, who has the superpower of flying through solid objects and rescuing anyone who is on the other side of those objects and might be in mortal danger.

They ask her how she liked working with the guy who stars in the franchise and was on their show a couple of weeks ago and who was funny as hell when they sat down and interviewed him. She says he was funny as hell to work with. Only she doesn't say the words funny as hell, she says he was "the same". With her accent it sounds much cuter. Finally they ask about her equally famous twin brother and what he's up to. She says she likes talking about Gustavo even more than she likes talking about herself. The hosts think that's a pretty good line. Her brother is doing a project called The Universe and Other Responsibilities and it's a romantic comedy and he's never done one of those before. "I can't wait to see that other side of him," she says.

Vicky and Glenn get a little bit elated when they hear their picture being mentioned on TV. "I didn't know Gustavo and Francesca Angelica were related." There's one spring roll left and Vicky cuts it in half to share.

"Thanks, Hon. I didn't know we were doing a romantic comedy. I thought it was a drama." He stirs fiber powder into his water. "Gustavo works at a homeless shelter. Where's the humor in that?"

"He falls in love with the beautiful community service volunteer. That makes it romantic."

Glenn is at the counter filling his plate with seconds and catching up with his wife when the entertainment people sign off and one of those spots for the local news team comes on with alarming footage of past weather disasters and police standoffs and street protests but they don't say a word about the fact that this is old stuff from the archives and viewers do not need to panic because none of this is happening now and they're just trying to imply that if it were happening now they would cut away from the regular programming and take you there immediately, and besides that they're a really nice bunch of news people.

Glenn always gets miffed. "Why do they do that?" he asks Vicky for possibly the nineteenth time in their lives. "They scare people to death. Somebody should sue them."

Before the soap opera starts at one o'clock a Trombo campaign ad comes on. It's the one with Trombo himself. He's doing the talking and standing on the shore of Lake Erie wearing a suit and literally cutting a giant band of red tape with a giant scissors. "My opponent," he says, "wants people to jump through all kinds of bells and whistles anytime they wanna put up a refinery or open a strip mine. We gotta get rid of all the red tape in America!" Trombo hurls the giant scissors into the lake and stands looking into the camera with his arms crossed. He approves this ad because what's the point of having all this land if we don't get everything we can out of it?

The Stovers are quiet and eating. They're glancing at each other just enough to see if anyone is glancing at anyone. Vicky is chewing slowly, which means she's thinking.

"Do you think we should go to Pennsylvania?" She's missing the opening scene of the soap opera. Spence is confronting Simone because he just found out that Simone is really Erika impersonating Simone and recently made love to him under false pretenses even though she, Erika, died at the end of last season and was buried in the family crypt.

Glenn is engrossed in the steamy dialogue. "Hmmmh? Oh, Pennsylvania? Oh, boy." He looks out the sliding glass door at the geraniums that are getting out of hand and taking over the sidewalk. "I don't know, Vick. Is there some way we can just, get the flu or something."

Vicky says she doesn't know how she can say no to Sigourney. "She has her heart set on it. She's so excited."

"I'm kind of excited, too. For Artie. It would be fun to be there when the old rascal becomes President. He'll ham it up, it'll be nutso, but—"

She frowns. "But what?"

"I'm tired. After we finish the picture I just want to sleep. I don't want to fly to Pittsburgh."

"I don't want to fly to Pittsburgh either, but I don't want to hurt my best friend's feelings."

They both look out at the adolescent ground squirrel eating their geraniums that are supposed to have a repellant property when it comes to ground squirrels.

TWENTY-ONE

"**I** won't."

"Don't be such a goodie two shoes."

"Be quiet, Andrea, the Judge is looking."

"Harry just turned around. He's shushing us with his finger."

"Look, this is the layout of the store. My new friend from community service drew it for us. She knows that store. She stole her engagement ring from there."

"Put that away."

"I'll tell the Judge it's yours, Danielle, and that you dropped it, if you don't help me with this."

"I'll tear your hair out if—"

"Shhhh."

"Now the guy pleading guilty to manslaughter is giving us a dirty look."

"Let him. I'll manslaughter you if you don't help me with this. I want that bracelet for my collection."

"Andrea, didn't you learn anything from this whole—"

"Yeah, I learned what a complete doofus you are, Kimberly."

"Well at least I'm not a thief. Anymore."

"Well you're gonna be my lookout if you know what's good for you."

"Ow! That hurts. She pinched me, Danielle!"

"You're a bully, Andrea."

"And you're a couple of losers, Danielle, and this is what I think of losers."

"Ow! Oh, you want to play it that way, huh? Well wait'll I—"

"Hey!"

"Aghhh!"

"Ouch!"

"Harry!"

"Ow, that really hurt, Porsha!"

"Well you slapped me ten times harder than you did in rehearsal, Rachel!"

"Well see how you like this one, Porsha!"

"Eeee!"

"Aghhh!"

"Sigourney, look out for—! Here, let me—"

"Oh, Vicky, this is disgusting!"

"Glenn, do something!"

"They haven't called Cut yet."

"Keep it rolling, Stan, you might get some really good shit."

"Shut up, Sierra, you want me to get sued for everything I own? Cut! Cut, for crying out loud!"

Glenn is still a little woozy. He is not quite himself yet, he is not doing much of a job of holding up his end of the conversation. Vicky is finishing talking about how nice Stan's wife is and what a nice wrap party she hosted and how sweet it was the way she saved the evening by getting Rachel and Porsha to be friends again and laugh about the little puffy welts they gave each other that morning before Stan yelled Cut and called for an early lunch break.

Vicky thinks Sigourney had a really nice time and seemed so happy and was so cute when she was a little bit tipsy on rum and coke and was hugging everybody and waving at Vicky's camera and she wishes Glenn had stuck to rum and coke instead of swigging that cup of Israeli wine. Glenn doesn't say anything he just makes the face he can't help making when his acid reflux strikes and won't go away without little pink pills.

Vicky is driving. She's taking one of the canyons home. At this hour the canyon is mostly deserted and they have the road to themselves except once in a while when somebody comes along with their high beams on and driving like they're participating in time trials and it feels like the chance of the two speeding objects passing each other without producing an instant fireball over the black hillsides diminishes with each revolution of their walloping tires.

Slumber sometimes rules over reflux and even over dark twisted thoughts and Glenn's head has found an awkward perch between the headrest and the passenger window. His open saggy mouth says something profound about the miracle of sleep. Vicky switches on the radio.

It's one of the syndicated public radio shows but it's one of the ones that Vicky's never heard because it airs in the middle of the night, at least that's when they air it on her favorite station. The program's called "Click" and it's from WTUM in Saint Paul and the basic idea of the show is to interview everyday people around the country who do jobs that no one's ever heard of, or thought of, before. It only takes a minute of listening to the show to know that this is a very thoughtful, well-produced show and that this is a show that Vicky, and even Glenn, would listen to more if they could and they could, theoretically, if they listened to podcasts but Vicky and Glenn have never gotten into the habit of listening to podcasts even though Michelle and Ryan are always sending them links to interesting podcasts. This segment of "Click" is about a guy who lives in Edison, New Jersey, and he's the guy who thinks up the brand names of new drugs for the pharmaceutical companies, sometimes even before there's a disease or a drug that needs naming. He's actually just an advertising copywriter but then he found this niche and he's the guy who came up with some of the more successful drug names that you see advertised on television. His credits include Floxaban, that popular inhaler for rickets, Symbatar, the new pill for heart palpitations, and Protraxin. For gingivitis. He actually seems like a pretty personable guy and the interviewer really seems to enjoy talking to the guy. They click.

When this segment finishes Vicky's coming down out of the canyon pass and curving through little foothills. It's the top of the hour and the news from Principal Public Radio comes on. "The news from Principal Public Radio I'm Poppy Clyburn. President Brown will travel to New Mexico today to campaign for Senator Elizabeth Merrill in her bid to succeed him in the White House in January. The two leaders will speak jointly at a rally in Albuquerque where they hope to underscore their legislative achievements the past eight years and their moderate policies as compared to Senator Merrill's opponent, industrialist Arthur Trombo. Trombo is in Oklahoma speaking today at the annual conference of POAPAC, the Pipelines of America Political Action Committee. At a rally yesterday in Wichita, he made these comments: 'Tin Lizzy Merrill is the worst Senator in the history of Senators.'"

When she hears the voice of Trombo Vicky sits up straight. She moves her hands higher on the steering wheel. Her fingers grip like she's hanging in air.

"She has the biggest mouth in Washington. She's so full of gas we could heat Butte, Montana for all of

January and half of February.'" You can hear the cheer from Trombo's fans at the rally.

Vicky slows down when the road flattens out and she comes to houses and yards and streets. The noise of the engine and the wind die down. There's a new quiet in the car. She turns the radio lower.

"Senator Merrill only responded by saying that the people of Montana deserve better than to be objectified and stereotyped by a man who looks at our precious land and sees nothing but bulldozers and dollar signs. The race for the Oval Office has intensified in recent days and Mr. Trombo has, according to some opinion polls, narrowed the gap and is trailing the veteran Senator by less than three percentage points. In other news . . ."

The trees and streetlights on the boulevard roll strange shadows across Vicky's face. She brakes gently and moves into a little turn lane. She stops and waits for the left turn signal. She stares at the stoplight. There's not a headlight or taillight anywhere in sight, she could turn if she wanted to, even the coyotes have called it a night. If the Stovers' neighborhood were on a heart monitor this is the place where the doctors would shake their heads and turn off the little machine that has gone all silent and black.

The green arrow comes on, Vicky turns onto their street. She pulls into their driveway. There's a loud snort and Glenn sits up blinking.

"We're home already?" he says.

22

TWENTY-TWO

The pizza could be a little crispier. That's what Morales thinks but he wants a show of hands from all his subordinate bodyguards to settle the issue constitutionally before he puts it on the record. It's five to four against the pizza and the guys in the majority hold up their drooping slices as proof. The guys in the minority are gulping the floppy ends of their pizza to destroy the evidence. The vote is taking place in the dining room so that Mrs. Trombo can't hear. She's the one that wanted fresh tomatoes, peppers and eggplant on all seven pizzas. She's always saying that her bodyguards don't eat enough vegetables.

The Secret Service guys took their pizza outside where they're watching the perimeter. It's drizzling so their votes would have been tainted anyway. Sigourney and Vicky and Glenn are eating in the den. The polls have closed in some of the eastern states and the network is starting to call some of the races. Sigourney is still on her first piece of pizza. She's still on her second bite and some of the first bite may still be stuck halfway down somewhere.

The IT person from Arthur's campaign is finishing her setup of the video conferencing with Trombo election night headquarters. She keeps apologizing to Sigourney and the Stovers for making them move when she has to string wires or plug things in. The news anchor standing with his big screen computer says that his network is now able to make a projection in New York and that New York has gone for Merrill and she will get their twenty-nine electoral votes. He pulls up New York on his giant red and blue map and shows the numbers and how the suburbs came through for Merrill by getting a bigger turnout than was expected and eighteen percent bigger than their turnout four years ago.

Vicky has the remote and she made sure that they're not watching the network that Trombo always watches and that he likes to give interviews to and trade sarcasms with whenever they have a little free time during their shows. Vicky's anchor guy goes over to the totals board and shows where Merrill now has fifty-two electoral votes to thirty for Trombo. Most of Trombo's were from Pennsylvania and West Virginia. Glenn makes sure that Sigourney doesn't lose heart by these early numbers.

"We knew we'd lose New York and Massachusetts, don't worry, all his big states are still out there." He gives Sigourney the same smile he used to give his kids when one of their two goldfish sprang to the surface as soon as the food flakes were sprinkled but the other goldfish just drifted around the little sea castle and seemed to be dozing. At a weird angle.

Vicky has her phone and is getting some of this on video. She watches Sigourney and doesn't let her own face reflect any colors or margins or numbers or predictions from the TV, only divine adoration of her friend who is sitting there dressed in a classy outfit and looking more like the First Lady that she might conceivably turn into.

Sigourney is calling and checking in on Arthur whenever she can get through. He's backstage at his

Trillium Banquet Hall and some of his adrenaline, and maybe some of his testosterone, seems to be surging into his phone and out of Sigourney's. Whenever she catches him between calls or briefings, she tells him how proud she is of him and kisses her phone with noisy smacks and says everybody in America loves her big Booboo Bear. It's possible her big Booboo Bear is a little high-strung at the moment, her side of the conversation gets defensive.

"No, Arthur, you know I wanted to be with you tonight. I know it's your big night. I am not a party pooper, I can't help it if the studio needed us for an emergency dubbing session. These things happen in movies. And I'm very good at dubbing, you should see me. Glenn had to be there, too. Okay, Spanky. Spanky says hi. That's not true, Arthur, I like Pittsburgh very much. I did not say it smells like feet, that was Barcelona. Yes, I have the neck brace. Yes I know you think it's sexy. It itches."

Now the network sends it to Trombo election night headquarters where Adam Trombo is standing in the back of the noisy Banquet Hall to give statements to them and all the other networks. First he has a written statement by his dad explaining why Sigourney is not there for election night. First he blows out a long mouthful of air before he reads: "Hello my loyal supporters. More than anything in the world, my beautiful wife Sigourney was looking forward to being here tonight by my side." Adam looks up from his memo and his nostrils flare like a red fox cornered by liberal hounds. He slowly shifts his eyes back to the document. "But, alas she is not here to share my triumph, possibly the biggest triumph in modern history. As fate would have it, she was rushing to go to the airport, fell down eleven stairs, incurred a serious injury to the cervical spine, and is temporarily out of commission. Doctors won't let her get on a plane. She even has a hard time going to the john. But, my incredible success tonight will be unimpaired. And, I have a little surprise for you, which you will see in a moment." Adam doesn't look up but he rolls his eyes so privately that none of the reporters or camera people look like they're sure if they just saw something or not. "My patriotic friends, we got this election sown up, I don't care what they're telling you on TV, I know what the real numbers are and it's heading toward a landslide, maybe an avalanche, for Trombo-Denby."

The IT person in Sigourney's den has her headphones on. She gets the three friends sitting together on the couch in front of the camera and when the neck brace is on properly and the hookup is ready to go live she counts down and then gives them the signal with her finger and five seconds later they can see themselves on TV on a huge screen on the stage in Pittsburgh where, behind Adam Trombo and all the reporters, the Trombo mob are squeezed in and twitching with nervous energy. The crowd is riveted to the Banquet Hall monitors with the Trombo-friendly network and its election coverage. They are already excited because they're seeing themselves on TV at the moment and when they see Sigourney and her friends sitting on her couch in California and blinking, they all raise their fists and cheer deliriously and the IT gal gets Sigourney and Vicky and Glenn to wave into the camera and the people wave back and whoop and whistle.

The reporters interrupt Adam Trombo and their cameras zoom in on the live image of his step-mother and her friends sitting on either side of her and being celebrated by his father's supporters. The younger Trombo turns around to look, and when he turns back to the cameras he is just a red stubbly widow's peak poking savagely into the upper left hand corner of America's TV's.

More polls are closing, Merrill-Wexler pad their lead with both sides chalking up the states that everyone expected to go exactly the way that they're going. Sigourney gets Arthur on the phone and he is telling her to stop worrying about dumb states like Louisiana and just to think about the smart states where he is crushing it. He hangs up because he says he wants to go call some election officials who he thinks might be forgetting about some of their small rural precincts where he spent half of his money.

Trombo-Denby win Governor Denby's home state of Kansas easily. They are closing the gap in electoral votes and taking the lead in key states. Vicky is yawning and drinking bottled water and fighting with her eyelids like they have little tiny six-ounce weights on them. She dabs her temples with drops of pristine water that people in Norway apparently didn't need. Sigourney gets a text from Arthur saying that he might come out and make his victory speech in a few minutes, after he comes back from the can. Vicky looks at Sigourney undecided between sad and terrified. Their knees are hugging. They both wear maroon. Glenn's pants are green. The couch is white.

Now the Merrill-Wexler ticket might come back and win, they take California, Mayor Wexler's home state. When Adam Trombo comes out for another statement to the press he accuses the major networks of manipulating the election results and calling the states that go for Merrill as early as possible and getting really excited about those states and purposely delaying any projections for the Trombo states and when they do finally call those states for his dad it's so brief you almost miss it and they do it with sour faces and hardly any adjectives.

Some swing states are still left uncalled. Neither candidate has a guaranteed path to two hundred seventy electoral votes. The bodyguards are sleeping in the dining room and living room. The Secret Service are sleeping in their black sedans in the driveway, under scattered showers. The IT gal is playing with her phone with her feet up in a recliner-rocker. Vicky is asleep with her chin on the heel of her right hand, Glenn is noshing nonstop on an alternating string of salty snacks and sweet snacks.

He has the remote and he is surfing. The waves beckon to him. Sigourney's TV and remote are several generations newer than what he and Vicky are used to.

The networks check in often with their reporters on the scene at both of the rival campaigns. In Pittsburgh country music is blaring and the Trombo crowd is still on their feet and upbeat. They are no longer distracted by the fact that their chosen First Lady is sitting on a couch in a far-off place where it's three hours earlier and twenty degrees warmer. If their attention wanders and they happen to glance up at the big video screen, they can see Sigourney fiddling with her neck brace with wide eyes and open mouth and an inner beauty that can't be tabulated or extrapolated but was made for cameras and big screens everywhere.

Glenn is burping. He has to burp quite often but he is an experienced burper and can swallow them instead of broadcasting them. Vicky's breathing is slow and even and her pink lips emit a little popping sound like Puh every four seconds. Sigourney is chewing on her right index finger and is facially pleading with the TV and all the anchor people to be kind. Utah goes for Merrill. She leads the electoral vote two hundred thirty-three to two hundred and twelve. Trombo wins Iowa by less than five thousand votes. Merrill takes Illinois and Alabama by double digits. Trombo wins Texas. He got 51.3 percent of Texans.

The networks are running out of states. It all comes down to Missouri. And Missouri can't make up her mind. She has big blue islands in a sea of red. No one knows if a blue volcano will spill out and bury the sea or if the sea will rise up and sink the islands in a red Trombo flood. Missouri's Secretary of State tells America that they will keep counting all night. The TV anchors take that news bravely. They're apparently trained to hold their yawning and eye rubbing until they're off camera. They thank the Secretary of State and ask him to keep them posted. The

Secretary of State seems to have a sense of humor, even if he missed dinner and bedtime.

For Vicky it might be her bladder or it might be the crunching sound from Glenn and a bag of grooved potato chips, some alarm goes off in her head. She gets up from the couch groaning and turns toward the nearest bathroom. The right side of her face is red and wrinkly. She stops. There's music on the TV. Fanfare music with horns. She looks at Glenn. His mouth is open for a large chip but he's not looking at the rugged chip he's looking down at Sigourney who has thrown herself onto her knees in front of the TV like she's auditioning for the helpless widow in a low-budget melodrama.

Missouri might still be counting but the networks have what they need. They can project a winner of the Electoral College. It's 11:30 pm California time and Arthur Trombo is the next President of the United States. Sigourney does a frightening inward gasp. Five seconds later she's on the couch weeping like a baby, using Vicky's chest and arms as a swaddling blanket.

Glenn is pumping his fists from side to side and yelling stuff like "Atta boy, Artie, that's my boy, Artie, Hell, yes."

"It's not even midnight," he gloats in Vicky's direction. Vicky looks at her husband in shock as she cradles her friend, rocks her gently and tells her everything is okay.

The IT gal is stoked. As soon as she can manage it she gets her three wards upright on the couch and doing their emoting in the direction of the camera. They can't see themselves waving and the crowd waving back unless the network sends it to Pittsburgh, but somehow the networks have a gut feeling that they need to send it to Pittsburgh very, very soon.

At 11:32 and a half Trombo bursts out upon his stage holding hands with Governor Denby over their heads. The two men wave their fists high and the loudspeakers start playing their victory song "Anything Goes" and with the country rhythm they thump their burly bodies at the crowd and the crowd is dancing and hugging and crying and collapsing on the floor in heartbreaking relief that they have saved America from the brink of a liberal apocalypse.

Trombo clutches the podium and leans very close to the microphone. The banquet hall drops into silence like someone pulled a plug. "All you pollsters, all you idiots, you said it was gonna be a nailbiter. You said it was gonna take days, maybe even weeks. You said every last vote would count. Well, whadya say now? Nailbiter my tuchus. This was a cakewalk. It's embarrassing how easy this was." He continues his remarks in similar vein, thanking everyone, including his sexy wife and his handsome son. He turns and looks over his shoulder at the big screen. "There's my beautiful Kitten now. Wave at the nice people, Sweetheart. That's it. How do you like your new First Lady, America?" The Pittsburgh crowd goes nuts. "Isn't she somethin? Even with a pinched nerve she makes all the other First Ladies look like my old piano teacher. Speaking of which," he says, pointing, "there's my old buddy Spanky. Whadya say, Spanky? Whadya think of your old partner now? Spanky's got his own gorgeous wife. Give us a wave there, Vicky. That's it, a little more. There ya go. Atta girl. Anyways, my friends, big changes are coming, and I mean big. We're gonna do things the American way, and we're gonna do things the businessman's way. I got a list right here," he says tapping himself in the head, "of all the government programs that are spending our money and giving us zippo for it. The first Department that's going on the chopping block, Trombo's official chopping block, is—"

At the Riverside Multiculture Center in New Orleans Senator Merrill comes out hand in hand with Mayor Wexler, both smiling and waving at their election night faithful. Their campaign theme song fills the auditorium.

"Cloud Nine" by the Temptations. It energizes the assembly but everybody in the room is beaming and bawling at the same time. The news people remark how the rank and file are way way more emotional than the candidates but since it's 3 am their time the news people are a little overwrought themselves and if the tears keep rolling like this there could be a new, salty tributary to the Mississippi by morning. Mayor Wexler stands to one side with a wistful expression. Senator Merrill gives her concession speech. Vicky starts crying almost from "My fellow Americans".

"Our historic march," says the Senator, without a teleprompter and when she's finally able to be heard, "a march for equality and freedom throughout our land, has not been fully successful. But." She puts a hand up before the audience has a chance to protest. "But. No no. I know. It's okay. It's okay. We have succeeded, we have succeeded, in making such strides, such courageous strides, that we need never think of turning back from our journey to a better tomorrow." She lets them cheer for a little while and blows out some air. She smiles at her running mate. "We have pushed the envelope, and that envelope holds the promise of renewable energy, more honest government, and the equal rights of all women." If you could only bottle the love.

"I hereby concede today's election," she says, when it's quiet, "and want to be the first to congratulate Mr. Trombo and Governor Denby on their victory. I pledge to work with the new administration to bring about reforms in health care, immigration, and trade policy, just to name a few. And I am hopeful that the rhetoric of this campaign will be left behind with the noisemakers and the streamers. That truth and moderation, rationality and respect, will be the hallmarks of the coming days." Senator Merrill thanks her supporters and campaign workers and gets choked up a little bit. There's a little blue hankie in her hand. It would have looked nice in Mayor Wexler's breast pocket. "It has been an honor to be your candidate and, although this was not the outcome we were all dreaming of, I know we will all continue our work to make our world cleaner, safer and more just. God bless you all."

Vicky is blinking a lot and sniffling but has to put on a brave happy face for her husband and her best friend who are suddenly starving and high on life and decide to go in the kitchen to warm up pizza in the microwave. Sigourney waves at the pizza as it goes around. Glenn thinks that's cute. Vicky's smile is the same kind you would get if you told Mona Lisa that you like her hairdo just as much as what they're wearing this year.

The bodyguards are still sleeping in the other rooms. They don't know that their lives have just turned, if not upside down, at least sideways.

23

TWENTY-THREE

Where did he go, Vicky wants to know. She's watching a video about how to knit a doggie sweater. Claudia is snoring by the fireplace they haven't used since the kids were kids. She would look nice in a green pullover.

He put out the garbage cans, he says.

Why didn't he wear a jacket?

"It wasn't that cold. But guess what I saw?"

"What?"

"Something I thought I would never see," he says.

Such a claim thirty-five years ago would have sounded pretty interesting to Vicky. But thirty-five years of Glenn does something to a person's zeal. Her face is prepared to be underwhelmed.

"I saw wild geese that fly with the moon on their wings."

"Ahh."

"It's a full moon over the Richardson's palm trees, they flew right across it. Maybe three or four of them, headed north. They were honking."

"Wow. Shouldn't they be flying south?"

"I think this is south for them."

"Are you gonna call Julie Andrews?"

"Maybe we'll sing a duet."

"Put her on speakerphone. I'll video."

"What time is it in London?"

"She's probably an early riser, I think it's okay."

"I wish you had been there to see it, Vick. We should always take out the garbage together."

"That would be nice, Sweetheart. We don't do enough things together."

"I've been saying the same thing since Labor Day."

"Silently. To yourself."

"Yes. But with a ring of sincerity."

"Do you think working on movies has changed the way we talk? I mean, have we always been this glib and witty?"

"Ha. I think we've always been pretty sharp, Vick."

"I feel like we're turning into Harry Met Sally."

His kiss disrupts a perfectly good Meg Ryan smile. Like the one where she met Harry.

Glenn hasn't worn flannel since he was a kid. Vicky says she likes him in flannel, makes him look like Jimmy Stewart in Anatomy of a Murder. She may be thinking of some other picture, maybe Seven Brides For Seven Brothers. Glenn isn't so sure about the flannel, he's twitchy. He's in the old oak rocker. He's facing the big bright window on the world and rocking and squinting.

Vicky's warmed up now. After two cups of cocoa. Sigourney was excited to make Vicky one cup of cocoa, let alone two. She says cocoa is the one thing she's really good at, in the kitchen. Now she's fixing coffee for the boys, if they don't mind instant.

Vicky tucks her feet up on the couch and unfolds the

quilt. It's a big puffy checkerboard of squirrels and birds and trees. Her cheeks are still rosy. She asks Glenn if he remembers the last time they went hiking in snow, he thinks it was Lake Arrowhead when the kids were around middle school and they stayed in that bed and breakfast with the soft boiled eggs in those little egg cups.

"I don't remember snow being this cold," she says, trying to get both shoulders fully encased in quilt.

"Honey, Lake Arrowhead is the tropics compared with here. We're as far north as Minnesota. Also we're fifteen years older."

"Thanks for that reminder. Dear."

"Some life these people have, huh? A place in the mountains just sitting here whenever you feel like it. View of Lake George out your window. Cute little Danish couple to keep it clean and spruced up year round. Man oh man. When he said hunting lodge I pictured a rustic cabin in the woods. Like in the movies. This is a four star hotel. All to ourselves."

"Until Adam and his family get here."

"Well they're family."

"Mmmmh".

Glenn isn't crazy about the idea of getting up early each morning and trudging out into the snow. But it's hard to gripe when Trombo sprung for their air fare and the weekend is costing him next to nothing. This is the second or third time Vicky has heard this philosophical monologue so far since they left L.A. She sneaks into the kitchen to take video of Sigourney reading the directions on the jar of powdered coffee.

When it's dinner the Danish woman makes them her special meatballs in curry sauce, roast beef on dark rye bread, pickled vegetables, and caramel egg custard.

"Bear and white-tailed deer. That's what we're after." Trombo is chewing a mouthful of pickled cabbage.

"Dad," says Adam, "when have you ever seen a bear up here?"

"Never, but I've never been President before, either."

The younger Trombo groans to his wife Kelsey. Their two little kids look at the weird food on their plates and look at their mother and father in panic and Kelsey Trombo leans over and whispers something reassuring about how Grandpa's just kidding and how there are no bears up here and they wouldn't eat them even if there were and even if they did eat them Mommy would tell them first before they ate them without knowing.

The Trombo men start a little discussion regarding choice of weapons. They discuss gauge and caliber and scope and trajectory. "Rifle, Spanky, or muzzleloader? Or you can hunt with bow and arrow if you want to. I've got Adam's old bows up here. Somewhere."

Vicky's eating has slowed down to a distracted nibble, she listens to the conversation like she's an undercover reporter from the New York Times at a strategy meeting of the KKK.

"I was a pretty good archer at summer camp, when I was a kid," Glenn says, avoiding Vicky's eyes. "I won the William Tell Award. At Camp Bigelow. Miss Weldon the Assistant Director said I had the perfect stance, she wanted to sculpt me in clay but I had to leave camp early with some kind of rash." Vicky shrugs with a face that had never heard that one before and doesn't quite see its point.

"I really seriously doubt that archery lessons at, at sleepaway camp qualifies anyone for big game hunting in the Adirondacks. Ulp." Adam swallows his last mouthful of bread and peanut butter, which is his dinner, and licks the spoon for his custard pudding. "But whatever. Go for it."

"Now that's not very supportive there, Sport. Don't pay Junior any attention, Spanky, he's just grumpy, needs a nap. You'll do fine with the bow and arrow. Hey, remember that time we made slingshots with sticks and rubber bands and cracked all the street lights on West

Ogle Street? I ditched you and you started to cry and couldn't find your way home? Your Grandma had all your cousins out looking for you? Man we had fun."

Glenn flushes and tells Artie that he's a big fibber and starts telling the girls that hardly any of that stuff is true when a Secret Service Agent in a green parka and wet boots looks into the dining room to see if everything is okay here in the lodge. He calls everyone Sir or Ma'am. He reports that everything is quiet around the property and they'll keep checking in periodically. He tells everyone to have a good night.

The future First Lady stands up when the Agent is there, she waves at the guy when he's leaving and tells him to have a good night too and calls him Officer. She looks nice in a blue sweater. "Arthur," she says when she's back in her chair and stuffing meatballs into a stretchy crepe, "we're so excited about tomorrow. Right Vicky?" She licks the sauce off her fingers. "Kelsey is taking us skiing, she hired a personal ski instructor to pick us up and take us home and spend the whole day with us." The girlfriends start giggling about the idea of getting up on skis for the first time and about how handsome the ski instructor might be and Sigourney tells Vicky how Kelsey Trombo and her little girl Gigi are amazing skiers and maybe they'll just watch them at the beginning but at least they should try the Bunny Slope and if anything happens then the handsome ski instructor will carry them home so maybe it would be worth getting a sprained ankle after all.

Arthur's cell phone rings. He answers it. He rolls his eyes. To his son he mouths the word Bolivia.

Sigourney whispers to everyone that this weekend Arthur has already gotten calls from twenty or thirty CEO's, a bunch of Governors and Mayors, Congress people, and the Presidents of Pakistan, Greece and Botswana. Trombo goes to his study to take the call. "Hello, Amigo. Well thank you very much. What's that?

Absolutely, you can come up to the White House anytime, any old time. Love to see ya. Mi casa su casa. Yes I'm looking forward to it too. No, you didn't wake me up. What time is it where you are? No kidding. Say you're a night owl, ain't ya? Ah, ha ha ha. I hear ya. Listen, Antonio, I wanna tell you that I appreciate the fact that your people don't come over to the States, you know, illegally. Like people from those other—. Yes it is a long ways. Oh I see. Uh huh, uh huh. Fine. Anyways, I just wanna say that you must be doing something right down there. Oh, ha ha. That's pretty good. So I was thinking that, you know, since we send quite a lot of dollars down your way and American companies invest a mucho lot in your uh, your economy, maybe you guys will pitch in and help us with our illegal immigration problem. How? Well maybe your navy could do something, you know, like—you what? You don't have a navy? Well maybe your army could do something, you know, patrol the jungles or something. Or you guys could just take a bunch of those illegals off our hands. You know they keep coming by the thousands and—Hello? Hello?"

"And the third thing I'll do is appoint a special prosecutor to prosecute Homer Brown for lying to the American people." The guy is whispering but it's stage whispering. It's like he has a built-in microphone and P.A. system in his esophagus. The Secret Service people are keeping ten yards back and ducking behind trees and glancing weirdly at each other and rubbing their purple ears and looking around for hidden speakers every time they see little warm puffs of fog leaving the guy's mouth. "Homer Brown called me a robber baron. In his last speech from the Rose Garden. That was—" He belches. The Secret Service flinch. "Damn that Annagreta and her oat bran waffles. How many did I—nevermind. Anyway, that was sheer Defamation, I've never been indicted for Robbery in my life. Illegal Dumping, yes. But not Robbery."

"Dad, your blood pressure. Also, you said one of the first things you would do is defund the Department of Education and the Department of Labor." Adam is stooping over a set of tracks in the snow and feeling the imprint with his bare fingers and then smelling his fingers. He frowns and aims a sharp glare in the direction that the tracks go.

"Oh that's right, Sport, defunding unnecessary crap is definitely the third thing I'll do. Hiring a special prosecutor is the fourth thing I'll do. And I'll hire the meanest bastard I can find, get me some names, will ya, Kid? I don't want no delays, I want that liar in jail by Valentine's Day."

"Artie, I see something over there by that tree. Is that a deer?" Everyone turns to statues. There's a halt in the crunching of dead leaves beneath the snow.

"Holy shit, you sighted a buck, Spanky."

"It's bigger than I—"

"Shhhh," says Adam. His rifle is directed toward the deer, more as a pointer than as an ultimate weapon. He uses his gun to wave the others down behind a fallen tree trunk with old snow in its cracks. The four hunters go to their knees and then their stomachs behind the dead pine tree. The two old guys are breathing hard, huffing vapor into the morning chill. Little Griffin Trombo has the muzzle of his tiny toy rifle in his mouth, is peeking over the log and is hypnotized by the velvety giant as it munches dead leaves and twigs from tall skinny birches and maples just twenty yards away. Arthur hauls his belly up onto the decaying timber and takes deliberate aim at the stag. Adam puts a hand around the barrel of his dad's shotgun "Not yet, Dad, wait. Til we're all set then I'll give the signal."

He joins his dad in shooting position. He helps his kid to take careful aim with the little replica, showing him silently how to close one eye and line up the sights. The boy is a good little soldier, holding perfectly still with face full of hope and promise. His tiny nose is running and his big corduroy jacket sleeve is wet and sticky.

Glenn has his station just inches to the left of the little Trombo enclave. He pulls an arrow from the quiver and notches it in his bow. The instrument is handsome and handmade, from Scottish wood. In color it matches the brittle plants and fungi growing on the old tree trunk. With his middle finger and forefinger Glenn cradles the arrow and pulls part way back on the string. He is shivering slightly. He closes his eyes and aims up into the trees, high above the unaware animal and the large spiky antlers. The Secret Service Agents watch from behind trees and rocks. They have their walkie-talkies on mute. Behind dark glasses they are deadpan.

The shooters wait. The only movement is a damp icy wind against their faces. It comes from the north, where blue mountains prowl the horizon. There's a dry swallow by Glenn and then a loud breathy whisper of "Now" and a second later the guns erupt like instant thunder. Glenn recoils and screws his eyes tight with pain. He lets his arrow fly upward.

There are hard voices swearing. There are uncertain sounds of something clashing down through the woods. There are little boy questions and two Trombos groaning and scrambling to their feet and Secret Service Agents stamping the ground and stretching to warm their bones. "Open your eyes Spanky your blessed deer got away how the hell did I miss him he musta moved at the last second. It figures. Somethin fell, though, I saw it."

Trombo puts down his gun and goes a few paces in the direction they'd been aiming. He bends down and picks up Glenn's arrow in some dead brush. He holds it up over his head and displays it in the bright air.

Something grayish and a little bit red is stuck to the end of the arrow.

"You killed a dove, Spanky. Got it right in the breast. Ain't Vicky crazy about birds and things? Man I wouldn't wanna be in your shoes, you're gonna be in hot water for weeks. Maybe months."

"How's she going to—" Glenn stops short with the look of someone who just answered his own question. The guy wielding the dead dove and planning to rewrite Article II of the U.S. Constitution is eight feet away and smiling at him.

When the pounding noise of the chopper comes it seems according to Sigourney's face and Vicky's face to be the sound of a huge meat grinder. Adam is airlifting the carcass of the large buck he killed late that morning, and a team of local butchers, to the lodge with his dad's helicopter. Even without coming anywhere near the unloading and slaughtering operation the girls are miserable and appalled, they keep telling the guys how disgusted they are with them and how their husbands have now managed to ruin the marvelous day of skiing and laughing and beauty and fun that they had been so excited to tell them all about until they heard about the poor murdered deer.

"Guess what, ladies? Spanky shot a dove. Right through the heart. His very first shot."

Glenn is looking at Trombo and getting red and his face is saying Gee thanks Artie, for once in your life you decide to be totally honest and it has to be now?

"It was an accident," Glenn tells Vicky, turning toward the fireplace. He tries to warm the half of him that looks fully guilty and knows it. Vicky can't speak.

She's as numb and frozen as that dead dove out there on that cold casual mountain.

TWENTY-FOUR

Arthur is mad. There's a little saliva hanging from the right side of his mouth. He's on his phone. He's in his jet. He's over some river valley in Arkansas, which has flooded. He's got a Club Sandwich on Focaccia on his lap. He's speaking with the Secretary of Homeland Security whom he's going to fire in twenty days when the Brown Administration moves out and the Trombo Administration rolls in. The Secretary seems to be enjoying the situation, while she still has her title. The madder Trombo gets the more charming she becomes, she talks to the guy like he's her four-year-old who just fell down and skinned his little knee.

He rages in vain. The Secret Service won't let him walk the red carpet, he's taken it up their chain of command and the Department is an unyielding wall of carbon steel. He's the President-elect. It's New Years Eve. And that's a security nightmare they're not willing to risk, the almost-leader of the free world is not going to get bumped off, not on their watch. The Secretary of Homeland Security refuses to countermand her agents,

Mr. Trombo will enter by army chopper, he'll get dropped off on the roof of the theater after the stars arrive by limousine and do their walk. The Secretary hangs up on him. She tells him that she has some actual national security stuff to work on.

The Westwood Lyceum Theatre doesn't sit modestly on a square city block like most retail structures. Rising up like a volcano in the Java Sea it's all by itself on a concrete atoll where popular diagonal streets come together. It's a glossy place and tonight looks even glossier than normal, and ghostly, under a steady drizzle where floodlights whirl and orbit upon the low clouds. The marquee says Tonight: World Premiere! Sigourney Trombo in: The Universe and Other Responsibilities! It says it three times, once on the side facing the street that goes to the campus and once on the side facing the street that goes to Wilshire Boulevard and once on the side facing the street that doesn't go anywhere, really, but just intersects with all the other bent little streets that make out-of-towners wish they had just stayed at their hotels and eaten in.

All three streets are closed off and by the time the starlet's husband lands and gets escorted from the roof down the emergency stairwell and into the theater, there's a frenzied shoving crowd all around the building and news cameras and microphones are expanding their own little universe. Movie fans have their phones and autograph books and Trombo fans have their shirts and hats and signs from the campaign. Anti-Trombo protesters across the street are trying to push the police back and get closer to the theater. They're wearing black and some are wearing gas masks and some are chanting "Stop. Your. Drilling." and there are signs about the atmosphere being poisoned and rising sea levels and children's lungs and disappearing species. Trombo's hair looks very red. His face is a bowl of milk of magnesia.

Inside, nobody pays any special attention to him. This is a crowd of show business types, it's not cool to be starstruck by celebrities. But everybody gawks like schoolgirls at the Secret Service people.

The Master of Ceremonies is Sid Rubio from Channel 6, the entertainment reporter who does all the red carpet broadcasts. He just says a couple nice things about why they're all here and thanks everybody for coming and then he looks up and gestures large at the screen and says "So, without further adieu" and says the name of the picture and then gets off the stage while the audience shows their enthusiasm and they show it loud but short and the theater is suddenly a dark vault of nervous, expectant silence while the guy makes his exit. It's quiet enough to whisper and Glenn asks Vicky how somebody gets posture like that.

After about eight seconds of high tension and low breathing, the crowd sees the screen light up and the picture is rolling. Everybody is glued. Nobody is touching their candy or their popcorn. They're laughing in the right places and sniffling at the right times. Their faces are little movie monitors. Stan the Director is beaming in the projected radiance. His wife is watching him from the corner of her gentle eye.

Trombo is restless, noisy, clearing his throat, looking around, Sigourney has to put her hand on the guy's shoulder several times to keep him still. Even during one of her best scenes. It's the scene where Kimberly's ex-husband comes after her with a harpoon and everybody in the audience jumps but she clobbers the bum with a series of kicks and punches from Tae Kwon Do because Harry gave her a pep talk in the previous scene about standing up for herself and she once dated a guy with a third degree black belt. The audience cheers.

At the end of the picture everybody's on their feet with a tempest of applause and whoops and whistles and even bigger outbursts during the credits.

"You were good, Dad." Some of Michelle's makeup is streaked from the scene where Andrea comforts a little kid in the cancer ward who's about to get his bone marrow transplanted. Michelle can fix her face before they go to the after-party.

"Yeah, Dad," says Ryan. "Who knew?"

"Don't sound so surprised, guys."

"What do you think of your old Dad, Kids?" says Vicky.

"Are you sure all this fame and glory isn't gonna change him?" Ryan's in one of Glenn's old sport coats. He's wearing a newsboy type golf cap to cover his waning hairline.

"He'll still be your boring old Dad."

"Thanks."

"You were great, Honey."

Sid the MC is back saying "That was amazing", "major blockbuster", "wowed big time" and other effusions.

"Yeah you were great, Honey," says Trombo snickering over Vicky's shoulder at his old chum. Sigourney is standing and pulling her co-star's arm because Sid is calling for another round of applause for the cast and crew and inviting them down to the stage for a few words. Glenn looks at Vicky and the kids for help and they remind him he's one of the main stars and he needs to get on down there. Sigourney leads him by the hand. He gets patted on the back a few times on their way down.

When they're all assembled across the stage Sid hands the microphone to the person at the far left.

"Hi I'm Robbie Nash and I played Rex." He hands the mike off.

"I'm Ellen Smitsky I was the Associate Producer." Everybody gets cheers but the audience has a few favorites from the picture like Sigourney of course and the guy who wrote the music and the actress who played the little homeless kid. After the introductions Sid approaches Stan and asks him why he wanted to make this picture.

"I guess I fell in love with the optimism of the script," Stan says looking out and up at the crowd. "The idea that friendship and trust make us stronger than any of the temptations in our lives. That there's a Florence Nightingale or a Mother Teresa inside each of us if we just open ourselves to those possibilities."

Bethany Bergil who wrote the novel and also did the screen adaptation and seems very happy and has a lot of energy talks about her vision, the struggle of young women in a materialistic society, the need for solidarity in the women's movement. She tells Sid she almost didn't make it to the premiere. Her car gave out on the Hollywood Freeway. She's a little embarrassed. "Did anybody else break down on the way here?" She looks down the row of flushed faces.

Glenn, at the other end of the stage, raises one hand about halfway. "Only mentally," he says. The theater has good acoustics and the audience giggles and Glenn will probably get credit in the papers for the best line of the night and everybody on stage seems to think so too and seem very proud of their Harry Filmore.

Sid can't resist coming over to Sigourney and asking her how she's feeling tonight, with everything that's happening in her life, and the celebrated beauty looks doubtful as he hands her the mike and she stares at it while she takes a deep breath and up in the middle of the theater Vicky sits blinking and catching the moment on video and Trombo sits up straight in his seat and looks around to see how many eyes are on him.

"Um—"

Sierra the 2nd AD is in the center of the stage next to actors and fellow crew members. She looks nice, all dressed up. You can still see some of the tattoos around her neck. Sierra is bending forward a little at the waist. One hand is against her forehead like she's shielding her eyes from the house lights. It's the hand that has large black Old English-style letters on each finger just below the knuckles. The letters spell HOPE. Sierra's voice when she screams is husky. It doesn't sound like hope. It sounds like terror. The words she screams are "Gun. Active shooter." Now the hand that says HOPE is pointing. It's pointing to one of the side exits. Where things are a blur.

"TROMBO SURVIVES ASSASSINATION ATTEMPT!!! Movie critics give the plot better ratings than the one in the picture . . .

By Frank Reingold, *Times* Staff Writer.

A sixty-four year old gunman is in custody this morning in Los Angeles for allegedly attempting to assassinate President-elect Arthur Trombo at last night's premiere of his wife's latest movie, *The Universe and Other Responsibilities*. Both the President-and-First-Lady-to-be are in good condition and are resting at their L.A. estate, having suffered only minor bruises in the aftermath of the attack. The suspect is being held without bail pending arraignment in federal court. Besides the attempt on Mr. Trombo's life, prosecutors will likely file charges for murder of a federal agent, the Secret Service Agent who took the bullet that was intended for the President-elect. The FBI has released a short statement on the identity of the gunman, who surrendered to authorities immediately following the assault: He is Dr. Sheldon Smith, an Anaheim, California, orthodontist who has been a loyal friend and advisor to Mr. Trombo in recent years. Investigators are still trying to sort out the suspect's state of mind and motive, but they have released a brief summary of the spontaneous statements made by the alleged assailant immediately after his arrest. It appears that Dr. Smith is a chief proponent of certain bizarre conspiracy theories, mainly relating to politics and the federal government. He reportedly told officers that an evil cabal that he identified as the Bureaucracy Beneath has kidnapped the real Trombo and replaced him with a lookalike imposter and that his intent was to eliminate the imposter and rescue the actual Trombo and thereby save our democracy.

The President-elect had no comment on his relationship with the suspect, but he did express some anger at the lack of security in a state like California that is controlled by the other party. He called for legislation making it easier for "all decent citizens" to arm themselves.

The film, touted as an Oscar contender in at least one category, is expected to be a big money-maker for West Coast Studios this fiscal year. Critics, however, may have little good to say about the picture, as *Times* critic Luther Brach writes in today's Arts & Entertainment section. . ."

25

TWENTY-FIVE

The Trombos and the Stovers all have new suits. They all look sharp. There's no rule about it but most people would say you need a new suit if you're planning on being inaugurated or your best friend is being inaugurated.

The guys' suits are dark gray, the girls decided on beige. But not the same designer. This is the first time Sigourney really looks like a First Lady, according to the way everybody stares like they're seeing some side of her that they've never seen before even though all her sides were plentifully revealed a number of times when she was a Playpad Kitten.

She invited the Stovers over for some pre-Inaugural coffee. The Stovers' hotel is nice but not as nice as Blair House where the Trombos spent Inauguration Eve.

They finish their coffee and then they get ready to leave for the traditional Inauguration morning church service and everything is festive and it's going to be a fun day and then Arthur gropes Vicky. He gropes her fast and he gropes her hard. He gropes her in the hallway of

Blair House that goes to the Lincoln Room where she went to take video and where he can push her against the smooth dark wood below the portrait of Grace Coolidge while his own wife is touching up her makeup and his old childhood buddy is using one of the gilded mirrors in the Drawing Room to apply sunscreen and the President-elect of the United States can feel that none of his fellow Americans will hear or see what he's up to an hour and forty minutes before his Inauguration. Except Vicky. He uses his big hands with their coarse reddish hairs. He crams those hands under her skirt and under her blouse and he says little seductive things to Vicky that he's probably seen in the movies and she is mangled and stung and disgusted and she finally pushes him off and runs down the hall until she finds a bathroom.

Glenn has to practically yell at her to make her go to the Inauguration, the Inauguration she was so excited to experience, she doesn't want to go. She says she doesn't feel well. Glenn can't figure out what's come over her all of a sudden, he says she looks like she saw a ghost and maybe she did, the house is a hundred and ninety-four years old.

In the limo from the church to the Capitol Glenn is a serious and puzzled prosecutor, he knows his witness is hiding something. They're riding with the Belgian and Japanese Ambassadors and their wives. Glenn has to keep his questions low and private. Outside the limo there's a cold wind blowing.

"Just tell me if something happened or not." He's turned away from the window. He's hunched over and his face and the sunscreen on his nose are five inches from Vicky's hair. Nobody's wearing their seat belts. "Just, just say it."

She shakes her head. She's looking at the floor of the limo which is blue carpet. The Ambassadors are discussing trips to South America.

"It's something I did?"

She shakes her head.

"Are you sick? Was it the alfredo sauce from last night?"

She's tired of shaking her head.

"Did you see a dead animal?"

She looks right into his eyes maybe closer than she has in years, like the word Hopeless is tattooed across her pupils in little red letters and she needs him to read it carefully. "No."

"Then what? Just—"

"He groped me, Glenn. And I want to die."

"He—"

They're on Pennsylvania Avenue at the Peace Monument. The caravan is stopped. Some of the limousines had to catch up. Part of the crowd can see them from the Upper West Terrace of the Capitol. They built bleachers there. There's a low roar. Glenn jumps out, Vicky says "No, Glenn."

He walks up to the limo ahead of theirs. The windows are tinted black, he can see himself in the reflection. He screams "Artie".

One of the windows rolls down, it's Trombo's face. He's holding a piece of paper with notes on it. A gust of wind grabs the paper out of his hands and sends it flying above this city where so many speeches are made and betrayed. He says "What the fuck, Stover?"

"Get out here, you slimy bastard."

Over her husband's shoulder Sigourney looks out at Glenn. She says his name. She is pale and scared like a kid who gets to see a favorite uncle turn into a mean drunk. She looks like there's a question in her throat but she can't make the words fit together.

Trombo opens the door and gets out. He stands there. He tells Glenn to go back to his limo. He calls him Spanky.

"If you ever touch my wife again I'll kill you. I swear to God I'll kill you."

"Go to hell you whiny loser. Don't tell me you didn't feel my wife up plenty of times on that lousy movie set."

"You are such a sick, disgusting, lying creep—"

Everybody gets out of the limos. In their new beige suits Sigourney and Vicky stop about twenty feet apart. They look at each other with the sadness and hurt that usually take a lifetime to accrue. The limousine drivers converge in the roadway and exchange excited paramilitary gestures. President and Mrs. Brown get out from the same door the Trombos got out of. Some of the major donors try to pull Trombo back to his limo but he jerks his arms away. Practically a squad of Secret Service stand by trying to size up the situation and keep the crowd off.

Trombo waves everybody to stand back. He puts both hands up and chuckles like he's decided to treat this whole thing as a little misunderstanding that they can all laugh about later over beers. Everybody breathes a little sigh and relaxes. Then without warning he shoves one of his large Secret Service guys headfirst into Glenn. Glenn starts chasing Trombo around the limousine. Glenn catches him on the second or third lap.

A retired guy who hasn't worked out much since law school and got C's in Phys Ed because he couldn't climb the rope in the high school gym can't expect to throw a knockout punch on his first try. Trombo's head whiplashes and he staggers a few steps but remains upright. Glenn is breathing hard. He looks disappointed.

Adam Trombo yells at Glenn. "Hit him again, the old lech." Which Glenn does. And Trombo topples at his feet.

"And don't call me Spanky."

It's a three minute walk to the Inaugural platform. John Roberts is there with a bible for Trombo's swearing and for Vice President Denby's swearing Clarence Thomas is there. He'll borrow the bible from John Roberts. And most of Congress is there and most of Wall Street is there and a college choir and a Navy band

and it's 45 degrees and overcast. Two thousand people bundled up and shivering and waiting for the next President of the United States to show up with a big wholesome smile on his face.

TWENTY-SIX

They brought back one of their former hosts from a decade ago. The last three or four hosts have flopped, in the minds of most people. People love her, she won't let everyone down. Her opening monologue is pure genius so far, she knows how to pick out the right subjects and stars and how to gently lampoon and strongly endear at the same time.

"—unless you're Leonardo DiCaprio," she says. That brings a big howl from the audience, any jokes with punchlines that end in certain celebrities' names are almost guaranteed to work with this crowd.

The seat fillers are busy. It's a restless crowd getting up frequently to go for a smoke, a drink, find a secluded bathroom. The Dolby VIP Lounge is jammed. But they drink their drinks fast and get back to their still-warm seats without missing too much of the excitement.

"Hey, did you hear that our new President wants to give a speech in Hollywood?" The big theater peals with boos. "Now, now. Give the devil his due." The audience loves that comeback, she loves their sensibilities. "The problem is, though, that he can't find a venue that will let him in. I feel bad for the guy." She holds up a quarter. "But there's a public toilet on Hollywood Boulevard and Wilcox and I'd be glad to lend him this."

In one of the front rows Sigourney is blushing and everyone knows the camera is on her and even though they're laughing at her husband they don't want to make her any more self-conscious than she has to be.

Pretty soon they do Best Supporting Actress and two former winners come out to read a little script and say the nominees and when they say "Sigourney Trombo for *The Universe and Other Responsibilities*" they show a little bit of the scene where Harry tries to stop Kimberly from telling off the Judge but she does it anyway and gets them both thrown in the slammer for Contempt. Sigourney is looking up at herself on the monitor with a hand over her mouth and giggling and Vicky is giggling and nudging an elbow into Sigourney's ribs. They both decided to wear their hair up. And look celestial.

"And the Oscar goes to . . . Lena Hathlebury for *Dust Motes in December*." Nobody seems surprised that this actress won and Sigourney looks relieved that she doesn't have to get up and give a speech.

Best Sound Editing goes to the picture about the dinosaurs that discovered artificial intelligence. Best Adapted Screenplay goes to *Das Kapital, the Movie*. Then they clear the stage and do a dancing and singing medley from the big musical set in post-war Guatemala. Then the host has a chance to get in a few more jokes about actors and directors and the funny things that have happened on the show so far and she takes quite a few commercial breaks from the sponsors that can afford to make special ads that are only going to run this one time during the Oscars and then get tossed.

Next up they announce the nominees for Best Feature-length Documentary Filmed and Edited Entirely on a Phone or Mobile Device, which is a new award category this year. There are only three entries in this category. One from South Korea, one from France, and from the United States, the film *Overtures: The Glenn Stover Story, a Man Who Stood Up When No One Else Did*. Vicky Stover, Producer.

Glenn has the remote. There's a cable attaching it to the floor. He turns up the sound and continues staring at the TV, blinking. The guy presenting this award is the guy who made that black and white documentary about motel toiletries. He tears open the envelope and says the winner.

When Glenn sees Vicky hear her name being called and look like she's just been slapped by invisible hands and bring her own two hands to her face, he blinks faster. He blinks while he watches Sigourney get emotional and embrace Vicky and rock her for a moment before she stands up, and while Stan and Sierra and other people from the picture smile and hug her as she goes toward the stage. She climbs the steps and the guy gives her her Oscar and leaves her alone at the microphone, and the clapping has stopped and nobody knows what words and what feelings are coming. She leans in to the microphone. She fidgets. She tries to figure out if she needs one hand or both hands to hold the statuette.

She starts by talking about irony. She looks at the trophy. Irony. How it shapes the stories we tell and the lives we lead.

"But stories don't have to end in irony," she says. "Sometimes we can turn irony into inspiration. Or integrity. Integrity is something that my husband, Glenn Stover, defines better I think than any other person in my life. I am in awe of what he has done and what he stood up for and I hope my film captured some of what I am feeling. How proud I am of the way he has handled both success and misfortune. That makes him the inspiration that has kept me going during these very dark times. And gives me the honor of thanking you for this lovely, restorative award." Vicky probably didn't want to choke herself up but it's probably one of those involuntary reflexes.

Glenn still has the remote but nothing needs adjusting. Maybe just the tightness in his throat and the moistness on his face. Glenn has the Day Room to himself. Except for the Warden. The Warden feels sorry for Glenn so he let him have the Day Room to himself during the broadcast. There aren't that many inmates that are allowed in the same area as Glenn anyway, though, since he's in keepaway status for his own protection, so it was just a couple ex-priests and a couple ex-cops who had to be sequestered.

Warden Gregory is standing and watching the broadcast from behind the couch over Glenn's shoulder. The couch is bolted down. Glenn invited the Warden to sit but he would rather stand. "I feel bad for you, Stover. I'm sorry you couldn't be there, you seem like a good guy and you got a beautiful wife that loves you." He looks up at the three photographs on the wall. Headshots. Smiling confidently. President Trombo and Vice President Denby and the new Director of the Bureau of Prisons, who is one of Trombo's buddies that he pardoned the first week he was in office. Warden Gregory shakes his head. Trombo looks the same in the picture, except his nose is a little crooked where it used to be straight.

"I especially want to thank my beautiful friend Sigourney Trombo, without whose encouragement and example I wouldn't be here tonight. And of course, my darling Glenn, to whom I pledge that I will free him and bring him to next year's Oscars."

Vicky is escorted off stage to the biggest cheer of the night so far and the Warden hands Glenn his handkerchief because unfortunately all of Glenn's are in the prison laundry and he can't get them until he shows up for his shift tomorrow morning at eight o'clock.

Claudia is barking furiously. She's at the sliding glass door seeing her own reflection. Vicky left the lights on in the family room. On the other side of the thick glass dusk is mounting in the dense backyard and the clamor of the big pooch sounds faraway. The light from inside creates stark shadows and reflections in the yard. The apple tree has leaves now but is clouded in darkness. The oleander is blooming, the geraniums are climbing the hedges and the dim light has rendered reds and greens and pinks all a drab gray. Faint cirrus formations streak the western horizon, the rest of the sky is a dark blue void. A cool breeze stirs the varied foliage and sometimes jingles one of Vicky's wind chimes.

It's time for the crows and the quail to roost for the night. A dove coos to mark the hour. In the pool a bee is losing its struggle against the surface tension of the water. Its little legs and wings are growing feeble, neither of the Stovers was here to rescue it.

Wrentits, scrub jays, spotted towhees are drowsing in their nests. Birds don't have to stay up late watching award shows.

Lizards and ground squirrels never have to wait up for election returns.

Dogs don't have a president.

www.ingramcontent.com/pod-product-compliance
Lightning Source LLC
Chambersburg PA
CBHW030412020726
47493CB00003B/1045